THE NERVIEST GIRL
IN THE WORLD

THE NERVIEST GIRL in the WORLD

Melissa Wiley

Illustrated by Mike Deas

Alfred A. Knopf · New York

THIS IS A BORZOI BOOK PUBLISHED BY ALFRED A. KNOPF

Visit us on the Web! rhcbooks.com

Educators and librarians, for a variety of teaching tools, visit us at RHTeachersLibrarians.com

Library of Congress Cataloging-in-Publication Data is available upon request.
ISBN 978-0-375-87038-5 (trade) — ISBN 978-0-375-97037-5 (lib. bdg.) —
ISBN 978-0-375-98902-5 (ebook)

The text of this book is set in 12.5-point Berling LT Std.
The illustrations were created digitally.
Interior design by Trish Parcell

Printed in the United States of America
August 2020
10 9 8 7 6 5 4 3 2 1

First Edition

For Scott, forever my leading man

Prologue

If I'd been a dainty little thing like Mary Mason, I would never have found myself in such a predicament. Mary was the kind of kid they always pulled in for deathbed scenes—sometimes she was in the bed, managing to look deathly pale and burning with fever all at once; and other times she was the devastated young daughter, crying her big old eyes out as Father or Mother murmured a last goodbye before croaking. Mary could turn on the waterworks as easily as shrugging. The second the director hollered "Action!"—instant Niagara Falls.

Me, on the other hand. I couldn't cry on cue to save my life.

But you'd never catch Mary Mason climbing out of a hot-air balloon forty feet above the ground.

I stared down at the patchwork world far below the swaying basket of my balloon. *Jeepers.* I was beginning to think that, this time, I might have bitten off more than I could chew. I was probably about to plummet to my death. Mr. Corrigan, the director, would probably just rush Mary in to blubber over my corpse while the light was still good.

"Go ahead, kid!" he yelled from his nice comfy spot on the ground. "It's now or never!"

"Never" sounds pretty good to me, I muttered, but only in my head because no matter how terrorstruck I was up there in that balloon, the thought of ruining a shot was eighty times more terrible. I took a big gulping breath of air—probably my last one ever, I figured—and grabbed hold of the anchor rope coiled on the floor of the basket. I heaved it over the side and braced myself for the lurch that would come when the anchor stretched the rope to its farthest point. I peered over the lip of the basket, but the rope was dangling directly below me and I couldn't see if the anchor had touched ground or not. It didn't feel like it. Too much sway.

"Now just shinny down the rope!" shouted Mr.

Corrigan. Even through his megaphone I could barely hear him, that's how high up I was. Far beneath me the scrub oaks danced on the yellow grass. A couple of crows zoomed past below, flicking their wings with effortless confidence. Show-offs.

"Just" shinny down, my aunt Fanny. Easy for him to say from his nice safe perch on the ground. But there was no getting out of it now. I had to get down from this balloon somehow. It was shinny down the rope or live in this basket for the rest of my short life.

I grabbed hold of the rope, scratchy on my sweaty palms, and said a little prayer in my head. I should have asked my grandmother who the patron saint of sliding down an anchor rope from a hot-air balloon was. *Quit stalling,* I told myself sternly, and flung a leg over the side of the basket. The only good thing about being so high above the ground was that nobody could see up my petticoats, but flashing my underthings to the crew was the least

3

of my worries. My hands felt so slick they might have been coated with oil. I wrapped a leg around the swaying rope, clung hard with my hands, and yanked the other leg over the basket.

The balloon lurched again, harder than before, and I nearly lost my grip. I squeezed hard and felt the heavy rope bite into my hands.

"Attagirl!" blared Mr. Corrigan. "Now give a good look around and then slide on down."

That *good look around* nearly killed me. Somehow the ground seemed twice as far away now that I was out of the basket. The nice safe basket where at least I wouldn't die from an overabundance of palm sweat. But there was no going back to that rickety little nest. My only choice now was to scooch down the rope and get to the ground as quickly as possible.

Well, maybe not that *quick,* I corrected myself. Falling to my death was probably the quickest way down.

Hand under hand, I inched down the rope. I could have sworn it took me an hour at least to make my way down that blasted rope, but I found out later it was only a few minutes. By the time I felt the anchor with my feet, I'd lost most of the skin on my hands, I had a big stripe of rope burn across my cheek, and my heart had burst with terror a good seven or eight times.

"Now, Pearl," shouted Mr. Corrigan. "You look down and notice the anchor didn't reach the ground. Give us a good look at your face—you're fearless and determined, remember—and then just jump the rest of the way."

There he was again with that *just*. I'd *just* like to see *him* jump down from the top of a tree with a fearless expression. I had to be six or seven feet off the ground still.

"She'll break a leg!" called the camera operator.

She'll break her neck is more like it, I thought, and let go of the rope.

Chapter 1

No one in my family had any thought of going into the pictures, not at first. We were ranchers—cattle and sheep, mostly, plus the ostrich enterprise. I heard about moving pictures from kids at school, but I never saw one myself until after I'd played parts in half a dozen different reels. By then my brothers were on their way to becoming stars—the Daredevil Donnelly Brothers, a Death-Defying Cowboy Trio. Which of course was a lot of piffle. Death-defying, my eyeball. They'd been racing horses across the chaparral since before any of them wore shoes—nothing death-defying about doing it on camera. Not compared, say, to leaping out the window of a burning building. But that's jumping ahead.

We lived outside Lemon Springs, California, in the eastern part of San Diego County. Our part of the county is thick with cottonwood, sagebrush, and yucca—heaven for rattlers and the occasional tarantula. My mother taught me to sit a horse at age three because she said it was safer than running around barefoot in snake country. By the time I was nine, I could ride as well as any of my older brothers, and I never had the benefit of trousers and spurs. I just hitched up my skirt and rode astraddle in bare feet. Why, I could ride standing up on the horse's back, holding on by my toes and the reins, if the terrain was pretty level—as long as I was well out of range of my mother's line of sight.

My big brothers' riding prowess is what got them noticed by the Flying Q director. They were working cowboys, and I don't think any of them ever imagined a life in the limelight. Once or twice a year they rode in local rodeos and usually snatched up most of the prizes; that was about as much fame as any Donnelly boy ever expected to experience. And then one day, a month after my eleventh birthday, a portly man in riding boots and breeches strode up to my oldest brother, Bill, after a calf-roping exercise, shook his hand, and said, "Son, how'd you like to pull that same stunt in a moving picture?"

"Huh?" replied Bill in his typically eloquent fashion.

"Name's Thornton Corrigan," said the man. He had a confident mustache and a kind of fierce snap in his gaze. "I direct moving pictures for the Flying Q Film Company. I'm looking for a couple of good riders for a Western we're shooting next week."

"Shooting?" echoed Bill.

"What's it pay?" asked my brother Ike, elbowing in. He was sore at Bill for taking first prize. Bill always took first in the roping events, but if there were a prize for getting straight to the point of a discussion, Ike would have taken it every time.

Mr. Corrigan didn't bat an eye at Ike's directness. "We pay handsomely for real talent," he answered smoothly. "I need fellas who can ride like the blazes and do some rope tricks on film—real showy stuff, plenty of panache."

"On film?" exclaimed Bill. "Like in the pictures?"

"That's right," said Mr. Corrigan.

"But we ain't actors," chimed in my brother Frank. He was sixteen, with one pitiful mustache hair for each year, more or less. I could see he was mighty impressed with Mr. Corrigan's bristle brush.

"I'm not looking for actors, son," replied Mr. Corrigan. "I've got actors crawling out of my ears." (I couldn't help but dart a glance at his ears then, even though I knew he was only being poetic. They appeared undisturbed.) "I need real cowboys. I pride myself on the authenticity of my pictures."

Au-then-ti-city, I repeated silently in my head. It was what my father would call a five-dollar word, and I had no idea what it meant, but I liked it. It sounded like a place I'd like to visit.

By the end of that conversation, Mr. Corrigan had gotten himself invited to dinner at the ranch. By the end of that dinner, he'd talked my father into giving the boys a day off their cattle work to do some rope tricks in front of a Flying Q camera. By the end of the week, all three of my brothers were roped into the motion picture business just as firmly as any calf Bill ever lassoed with his eyes closed, and my father had to advertise for some new ranch hands.

Chapter 2

Everyone around here thinks of life in two sections, like a two-reel picture: before Flying Q and after Flying Q. My mother tells me stories about how her family moved from Fletcher, Colorado, to San Diego, California, when she was a little girl, about as old as I was when the studio set up operations in Lemon Springs. She says all her memories are divided into Before The Move and After The Move. I guess it'll be the same for me, only it's Before The Movies and After The Movies. We stayed put on our same old ranch, and I still have to get up and do my ostrich chores before breakfast, same as ever, but just about everything else in my life is different since Flying Q swooped in. I guess when I'm old like my mother, I'll be telling my kids before-and-after stories, too. Assuming I don't break my neck jumping onto a moving train first—or get kicked in the head by an irked ostrich.

Our ranch runs mostly to cattle, but we have one big pen beyond the kitchen garden for the ostriches. We raise some for meat and some for eggs, and all of them for their big plumy feathers, which fetch a pretty penny. Mama sells them to a hatmaker in San Diego every year after molting season.

We keep six or seven birds at a time, most of 'em females because we rely on the eggs. One ostrich egg makes a scramble big enough to feed our whole family. Chicken eggs taste a heap better, though. My grandmother says chicken-egg scrambles are for fancy folk who have time to spend all day cracking shells. But I notice it doesn't take her all day to crack chicken eggs when she's making a cake. You'd have to make ten cakes if you wanted to use an ostrich egg. The only catch is that ostriches, unlike chickens, don't lay eggs year-round.

Here's what your morning's like when you're the youngest kid in the family, meaning you're the one stuck tending the birds. They aren't like other ranch stock—no chummy nuzzles like you get from horses,

or placid indifference like cows and sheep. No, ostriches are nasty-tempered she-demons who'd as
soon crack your skull as look at you. At least, that's
what my father says. He won't go near the birds.
"They're my wife's enterprise," he always says. She
grew up ducking kicks from the she-demons, just
like me—After The Move, that is. That means she
got kind of a late start, compared to me. I started
feeding the birds and collecting their eggs when I was
six years old. They mostly ignore me now. Ike says
I'm so gangly and long-legged myself that they just
think I'm one of 'em.

But I still have to look sharp when I open the gate to their pen or Jezebel will charge me. She's the meanest she-demon of the bunch. The trick is to fill their food trough first, then unhook the latch to their coop with a big stick poked through the fence, and then, after they've thundered out to bury their heads in breakfast, I creep around to the pasture gate and open it while they're occupied. After they eat, they stampede out to pasture and I use my stick to shut the gate behind them. Then I can clean the coop and, in egg season, check for eggs in peace and quiet. Well, quiet at least. It's hard to feel exactly *peaceful* when you're shoveling fresh ostrich dung.

When I'm finished, I carry the eggs into the kitchen, where my grandmother takes them over. I get sent to wash up before breakfast. Nobody wants to sit down to a meal next to the girl who cleans the ostrich pen.

It all goes in reverse in the evenings, except for the egg-gathering and poo-shoveling parts. Mama still makes me scrub my arms, face, and feet before I'm allowed to sit down for dinner. I used to think I must be the cleanest kid in San Diego County. Then I got to know Mary Mason. She bathes as much as I do (more, since her baths are long soaks in a tub instead of hasty scrub-downs with a rough towel like mine), and she doesn't get herself stunk up doing ostrich chores in between.

From our ostrich pen you can look east over the valley to Bittercreek and the mountains beyond. The sun shoots over those mountains in the morning right in time to jab my eyeballs with rays when I'm tending the birds. It sets over the Pacific Ocean, but we're almost twenty miles from the coast and our ranch is too flat for a view. Once, when I was six or seven years old, my father took my brothers and me to the top of Mount Caracol, a smallish mountain a little northeast of town, and we took in the view to the west, past Lemon Springs to San Diego and, beyond that, a glittering stripe of ocean. Papa lifted me onto his shoulders so I could see even farther. I remember how far away everything seemed—the ocean, the tall palm trees, the hills; even my brothers standing beside us seemed a long way down from my perch.

From our ranch the westward view is mostly just pastureland and scrub. In the mornings a fresh, clean smell of sage sweeps across the chaparral, and the comfortable sound of cattle drifts across the pastures. Every spring the spiky yucca plants send up tall shoots of big white bell-shaped flowers. Grandma calls them our-Lord's-candle plants. My brother Ike calls them hell's bells, because the yucca leaves are sharp as needles and will slice your arm if you get too close, walking by. (But he never calls them that around our grandmother.)

Until Mr. Corrigan appeared in our lives, I didn't think much about the world beyond our ranch and Lemon Springs. My world was ostriches and horses, and the rumble of cattle and the bleating of sheep, and school in the village, and Sunday Mass at the white stucco chapel. It felt pretty big to me, back then—before Mr. Corrigan sent me up in a hot-air balloon and I saw our ranch way down below, looking about as big as a quilt square.

When my brothers started riding horses in Flying Q's one-reelers, no one (least of all me) ever dreamed I'd wind up in pictures myself. I would bet a nickel my mother would have shut me in a closet before she'd ever let me near Flying Q, if she could have foreseen the crazy things I would wind up doing. I might have shut my own self in a closet if I'd known I'd wind up climbing out of a hot-air balloon forty feet above the ground.

I'm glad we didn't know.

Chapter 3

"Ike got shot off his horse yesterday," said my brother Bill through a mouthful of egg, about a week after the boys started working for Mr. Corrigan.

"Good heavens!" cried my grandmother, her fork clattering to her plate.

"Just pretend-shot, Grandma," Ike assured her. I don't know why she was so worried in the first place. If you've been *really* shot, I don't think you sit down at the dinner table nice and casual and snatch the biggest piece of ham off the platter.

"For the picture," Bill added superfluously.

"That was a splendid tumble you took, Ikey," said my brother Frank admiringly. "I thought you'd broken your neck for sure."

"GOOD HEAVENS!" shouted my mother and grandmother in unison. My father slowly set down his mug, eyeing Ike appraisingly. Mama rose hastily to her feet, her chair scraping on the floor, snatched up the coffeepot, and stormed into the kitchen. Frank stared after her with an anxious gaze, but Ike went on shoveling scrambled eggs and fried ham into his face.

"Why's everyone in such a stew?" asked Bill.

"Suppose," said my father slowly, "you tell us exactly what it is this fella Corrigan has you boys doing out there." In the kitchen a pot clanged hard on the iron stove.

"Aw, it's swell, Papa," said Ike eagerly. "Mostly, we ride hard in a pack of other cowboys and wave shotguns around—don't worry, they ain't loaded—but whenever the picture calls for a fancy stunt, Corrigan has me or Frank or Bill do it. We can outdo those other fellas by a mile."

"Don't boast, Isaac," snapped Grandma. Her mouth was pressed into a tight thin line.

"It ain't boasting, Grandma," said Ike, brushing a brown curl off his forehead with the back of his hand. "It's the plain truth. The rest of 'em can ride all right if the terrain's level, but if you need someone to take a spill or switch horses in the middle of a hard gallop—"

"Ike," muttered Frank in a warning tone, but Ike ignored him.

"—then you want a Donnelly on the spot."

"What the blazes kind of picture *is* this?" demanded Papa. "Sounds more like a circus act."

"Jesus, Mary, and Joseph," interjected my grandmother, making the sign of the cross.

"They're Westerns, Papa," said Frank. "That's why these picture people came looking for rodeo champions. It's a display of horsemanship."

In the kitchen my mother snorted. I couldn't help but let out a snicker. Ike shot me a glare. I quickly blanked my face and busied myself spreading manzanita jelly on a biscuit.

"Mm-hmm," murmured my father. I could see he was skeptical.

I spooned another dollop of jelly on my biscuit, figuring everyone was too distracted to notice.

"Shucks, Papa, you're the one who taught us how to take a spill without breaking a bone," Ike pointed out.

"That was a safety precaution," Papa snapped. "Everyone takes a tumble now and then. Best to know how not to get yourself killed. I sure as heck didn't expect you'd be going out of your way to fall *on purpose*, though."

"Jacob, language!" said my grandmother. My brothers all burst out laughing—it was always so funny when Grandma scolded Papa like a naughty child, especially since she was Mama's mama, not his—and I took advantage of the distraction to sneak another spoonful of jelly. I didn't have much biscuit left at this point, and the jelly slid down around the edges onto my fingers.

"That's too much jelly, Pearl," said my mother sternly. I always forget she has the eyes of a hawk and can see through walls. She stalked to the table with a fresh pot of coffee and slammed it down in front of Ike.

"Piggy Pearl," teased Ike. Frank made an oinking sound, earning a glare from me. Frank's teasing always had a different flavor, somehow, from Ike's. With Ike, you felt like you were in on the joke. With Frank, you weren't quite sure he *was* teasing. Maybe he really did think I was a pig.

"Don't you try to change the subject," Papa told Ike. "I need assurance that this work isn't putting my sons in danger."

"We're careful, Papa," said Frank. "The whole point is he brought us in because we can do tricks without breaking a sweat. It's nothing out of the ordinary for us, but I guess it looks tip-top on camera."

"Plus, the pay's fine," said Bill placidly.

My mother rolled her eyes. "The pay'll do you no good if you're dead of a broken neck."

"Just wait'll you see the picture, Mama," said Ike. "You'll be bursting with pride."

"Hmph," my mother said, unconvinced. "Pearl, go wash the jam off your face. You look like you took a bath in it."

"Yes, ma'am," I sighed. Ike gave me a wink. He's my teasingest brother, but also my most sympathetic one. Whenever I get into a scrape, he's the best person to ask for help getting out. I do blame him, though, for my lifelong horror of caterpillars because of the time he climbed a tree and dropped a nasty spiky one on my head as I walked underneath his branch. Of course, that was a long time ago and I was just a little kid—but some things you never forget, and the feeling of a million scrabbly little legs on your head is one of them. The oozy splat after you clap a pan-icked hand to your head is another.

But as long as there were no caterpillars in sight, Ike was a swell brother. Anyway, he was practically grown up now, almost eighteen, and not likely to ter-rorize me with creepy-crawlies anymore.

I don't think.

"I believe I'll ride to town this morning and take a gander at this 'nothing out of the ordinary' with my own eyes," said Papa. My brothers exchanged uneasy glances but said nothing.

"You just watch out that smooth-talking Corrigan man doesn't rope you in too, Jacob," said my grand-mother. "That man's so slick he'll have you dancing a tarantella on horseback if you don't keep your wits about you."

The image was so comical I couldn't help but burst out with a hoot of laughter. Ike met my eyes, grinning.

"*I said go wash up, Pearl,*" roared my mother. I hastily scooted out of my chair and went out to the pump to wash. But not until I'd licked up every smidgen of jelly I could reach with my tongue. It's a sin to waste good manzanita jelly.

Chapter 4

As I was drying my face on my shirt—which in hindsight maybe wasn't the best plan, because I wound up smearing some jam from my shirt onto my face—Papa and the boys strode through the courtyard on their way to saddle their horses. The boys were heading to Lemon Springs straightaway, but Papa said he'd follow later, after he saw to a few chores. I hurried through my own chores and then pelted to the sheepfold, where Papa was mending a gate while the ewes and lambs were out to pasture.

"Can I come along when you go to town?" I asked, trying for just the right note between pleading and nonchalant.

"What's the matter with your face, Pearl?" Papa asked.

I quit trying for any kind of facial expression at all.

"Ostriches set?" Papa queried.

"Yes, sir."

"Eggs?"

"Two this morning—Cleopatra and Bathsheba."

Papa considered a moment. "Well, I suppose Apple could use a stretch. If your mother doesn't need you."

I broke into a grin. Apple was my favorite horse. She never cared where we went, so long as we were going somewhere. Unlike Dinah, who always had strong opinions about which direction to travel— usually the opposite of the direction you needed to go.

"I'll be finished here directly," Papa continued. "Why don't you go saddle up and meet me by the bell."

I scurried to the stable, taking the long way around the house instead of cutting through the courtyard, where Mama was watering the grapevine. Papa's *yes* was no guarantee you wouldn't bump into Mama's *no*. It was exasperating, sometimes, to have so many opinionated grown-ups (almost as opinionated as Dinah) weighing in on every little thing. Between my parents, my grandmother, and my three grown-up brothers—at least Frank considered himself grown-up even though he was only sixteen, because he could ride cattle as well as Ike, who was seventeen, and Bill, who was almost twenty—I could hardly take three steps without someone bossing me or scolding me or both. I'd have given my left arm for a little sister or brother I could boss around myself. Well, maybe a couple of fingers off my left hand. Not the thumb; I needed it for holding reins.

Jasper, the stable hand, helped me get Apple saddled and ready. I hitched myself up onto her back (I could boost myself up from a stirrup if I needed to, but it was more fun to climb the rail fence and scramble into the saddle from the top rail) and trotted to meet Papa at the bell.

Our bell is famous in San Diego County. At least, the post it's mounted on is famous. It's a big weathered timber salvaged by my grandfather from a shipwreck in San Diego Harbor way back in 1856, before my papa was born. My grandfather used other wood from the ship to frame parts of our house, which has whitewashed adobe walls and long, low windows. When I was little, Frank told me you could hear the ocean if you put your ear to a knothole in the bell post, but when I tried it, all I heard were my own yowls when I got a splinter in my earlobe. Frank laughed and said I ought to try it with the other ear, too, and then I could wear dangly earbobs in the splinter holes. Sometimes I think Frank is like having an ostrich for a brother.

⁓

Papa beat me to the bell. He gave me a nod—he was never much for talking on horseback—and led the way along the dirt path rolling out of our ranch across the chaparral. The morning air smelled of sagebrush and honeysuckle, fresh and sweet. A lizard skittered out of the path away from the horses.

The path curved along the shoulders of a low hill. As we crested the hill, I turned to see our ranch spread out below. I always loved to see it from this spot because you could look down at the gleaming white walls of our house, which has three long, straight wings wrapped around a big open courtyard, with a high garden wall making the fourth side of the square. Our bell stands in the trampled, bare-earth space between our front wall and the stable. From the hill you can see the tops of the fig and orange trees in the courtyard, a rustling roof of green leaves surrounded by the curved red roof tiles of the house.

The boys had said they were filming in town that day. Our place was four miles from Lemon Springs, an easy canter in dry weather. The road that curved out of our ranch ran for a time along the edge of the plateau with a view of wide, flat plain below. Beyond the valley with its scattered ranches and scrubby pastures, a border of low hills melted into the bright sky.

Our path skirted a canyon lined with sagebrush and scrub oaks, then wound between hills toward town. Small birds flitted in and out of the manzanita bushes on either side of the path. My heart felt jumpy with excitement. I hardly ever got to town when school was out. Town meant a soda at the fountain on Straight Street, and the thrill of the train sliding into the depot, and maybe, if I was lucky, a good close-up look at an automobile.

We found my brothers on Straight Street, in front of the Methodist church. Straight Street runs straight through Lemon Springs, which is how it got its name. Most of the other streets in the village coil around hills or snake along the edges of canyons. All the most important buildings in town live on Straight

Street: the post office, three churches (including St. Francis, where my family goes to Sunday Mass), a soda fountain, a bank, and (best of all) a livery stable. The streets and lanes crisscrossing Straight Street are scattered with houses and gardens and a few buildings not interesting enough to live on the main road, like school.

The Methodist church is a plain board building with a gray spire. In my opinion it's not half as pretty as St. Francis, which is made of thick white stucco like our house. The fat walls of our church collect sunshine on sunny afternoons and save it up for the gray mornings of May and June, when clouds roll in from the sea. Grandma calls it May Gray and June Gloom—the heavy, dark sky of a spring morning that burns off to a dazzling blue in the afternoon sun. My favorite time to go to Mass is on a June Gloom morning because the stucco seems to glow with a soft light. Also, you can almost always find an alligator lizard running along a wall or perched on a fence rail, watching the world sideways with its little round eyes on either side of its head.

I don't know how many lizards loaf around the Methodist church on a regular day, but I guessed today they'd be hiding under the bushes, scared out of their little lizard minds. The street in front of the church was swarming with horses and people. It looked like Papa and I weren't the only folks who'd come to watch this moving picture business in the making.

My brothers were decked out in fringed jackets and gleaming white hats, sitting tall on their horses alongside some other fellows. Their eyes looked strange, like someone had smeared thick black paint around the lashes. A man with heaps of wavy hair beneath the gleamingest, whitest hat of them all sat on his horse a little in front of Bill and the rest of the cowboys. Mr. Corrigan was jabbering at him a mile a minute.

"At first you don't see Nell behind Bart, you just see him sneering at you, and you're going to raise your gun and aim right between his eyes. The audience will worry you're going to shoot clean through him and get the girl as well. The rest of you, don't draw your weapons; just keep your hands ready over the holsters. You know Jack can handle Bart by himself; you're just on the lookout for tricks. Nell, turn your head toward the camera. You're terrified; you're sure you're done for. Everyone got it? All right now . . ."

Mr. Corrigan moved to the side and I got my first

look at a real moving picture camera. It was a big black box set on tall, spindly legs.

"I'd like me a closer look at that," Papa murmured. He loved contraptions and machines of all kinds.

"Can I help you folks?" asked a young man in spectacles, appearing at Father's elbow. Hickory shied a bit and Papa had to pull hard to settle her down. Didn't this fellow know not to sneak up on a horse?

"Those are my boys," said Papa, nodding toward the cowboy gang. "I wanted a look at what's been eating up their time. Had to hire me a couple of hands since my best horsemen are trotting off to make pictures every day."

"They are fine horsemen indeed," said the young man eagerly. "Mr. Corrigan is happy to have them. Now we must hush—they're about to roll film. You may stand back here and watch, but take care to stay still. Don't let your horses move forward where they might nudge into the shot."

A man wearing his cap backward so that the beak covered his neck was peering into a hole in the box. Mr. Corrigan stood beside him, holding a long cone-shaped gadget.

"What's that, Papa?" I asked.

"A megaphone," Papa whispered. "You talk into

the small hole and it makes your voice carry so you can be heard by people some distance away."

Just then Mr. Corrigan lifted the megaphone to his mouth and shouted, "Camera!" At least, it sounded like shouting. The man with the backward cap began turning a crank on the side of the long-legged box. My brothers sat up even taller on their horses, squinting their darkened eyes into the sun.

"Action!" yelled Mr. Corrigan.

The fellow he'd called Bart gave his horse a light kick to start it walking. He rode forward slowly toward my brothers and the wavy-haired man. A youngish woman sat behind Bart sidesaddle, with her legs and head turned toward the camera. She had masses of long ringlets cascading over her shoulders, and her eyes, too, were outlined with black. She held them open very wide, which made her look a bit like a startled ostrich—but a pretty one. Her brows drew together and her mouth made a kind of O shape. She did look terrified, like a train was barreling down on her. Bart glowered at the wavy-haired man, Jack, and Jack and the other riders glowered back. Ike glowered so hard I thought his eyebrows might pop off. I had to bite my lip hard to stifle a laugh.

Jack raised his pistol and aimed it right at Bart. Bart gave a contemptuous laugh and said, "I'd think twice before shooting if I were you."

Jack cocked the pistol. He was aiming right at Bart's chest, and from where I stood I could see the bullet was going to go straight through him to Nell's head. She was clutching Bart around the middle, and you'd think Jack would have noticed she was sitting right behind Bart, but I guess not.

"I warned you," Jack said. Nell squinched her eyes shut tight.

Jack's finger began to move on the trigger.

"Don't shoot!" I hollered. "She's right behind him!"

Bart whipped his head to look at me, and in a flash I realized what a ninny I'd been.

"CUT!" roared Mr. Corrigan. He wheeled around to face me and there was thunder in his expression. Every single person there turned to look at me. It didn't help that I was perched high up on horseback in plain view. I had an urge to slide off and hide on Apple's far side.

Some of the cowboys burst out laughing, but my brothers looked confused (Bill), sympathetic (Ike), or disgusted (Frank). Nell rolled her eyes heaven-ward. Jack, the handsome hero, looked like he'd like to tar and feather me, but the evil Bart was grinning ear to ear.

"What in tarnation!" demanded Mr. Corrigan. "What were you thinking, kiddie? You wrecked the shot."

"I'm sorry," I croaked. I realized I was staring at my feet, wishing the earth would swallow me whole. "It just seemed so real for a second. I was afraid he'd shoot her."

Mr. Corrigan's bristle-brush mustache twitched. The corners of his eyes went crinkly.

"Seemed real, did it?" he repeated. "Well, that's a pretty good endorsement. If the audience reacts like you did, I'll call it a good day's work."

"Mighty sorry about that," Papa said. "I came to watch the boys, and Pearl wanted to tag along."

I felt my cheeks burning hot. Papa made me sound like a little tyke, or a pesky dog. I saw Frank roll his eyes.

"Don't trouble yourself about it," said Mr. Corrigan cordially. I guessed he didn't want to annoy Papa and risk losing his star riders. "You folks are welcome

to watch—as long as you don't distract my actors."
That last part was directed at me.

"Yes, sir," I murmured. I clapped my hands over
my mouth, just to be safe.

Mr. Corrigan laughed and turned back toward the
actors. "Let's take it right where we left off. Ready?
Roll it!"

Jack's gun was up and aimed again. "I warned
you," he said. The trigger began to move.

"Don't shoot!" cried Nell from behind Bart's
back, facing toward the onlookers instead of Jack.
As she spoke, she unlocked her hands from Bart's
waist and waggled them in a sort of frightened man-
ner. Jack's eyes went wide with surprise, and all the
cowboys looked like they might fall off their horses
in shock. Nell leaned to the side so Jack could see
her. He lowered his gun and put his other hand to
his heart, like he was about to faint or something.
Bart threw his head back and laughed a big openmouthed laugh.

They all looked a bit silly, clowning it up so
much. I had to press my hands extra hard against
my mouth to keep from snickering. Nobody had
told me the audience couldn't hear anything in a

moving picture. There would be cards with words on them to show what the characters were saying. But the actors spoke out loud anyhow, to make it all seem more real.

A little *too* real, if you asked me.

Chapter 5

After that, I was hooked, and so was Papa. "Finish your chores quick, Pearl," he would say, and I'd know that meant we were going to watch the boys at work again. I don't know why Papa bothered to tell me to be quick—I always finished my chores way before he did, even counting the after-ostrich washup. But then, what Papa had to do was less like *chores* and more like an *occupation*. We own a big spread with a creek cutting through the middle, lined with cotton-woods and sagebrush. Most of our land is fenced for cattle or sheep pasture, with a few grain fields, a big vegetable garden, and a small citrus orchard. In our courtyard we have Mama's grapevine, a couple of fig trees that Grandma pampers like newborn babies, and a lot of manzanita bushes with their tasty berries.

But our main crop, Papa says, is fences. As a rancher he's required by law to keep his grazing cattle fenced in so they can't wander onto neighbors' crop-land. Papa spends a heap of time inspecting the fence lines for breaks, or chopping rails, dragging rails, hefting rails into place. And then of course there's all the work of tending the livestock. Even with a team of hands, it's a mountain of chores. Especially now that his best hands, my brothers, had been swept into the picture-making business.

Frank, who has a knack for explaining the back side of things you only see from the front—providing you can put up with his delivery, which is like a learned professor talking to a very stupid child—told me it took about a week to film a story, sometimes less. The crew went all over our part of the county, shooting scenes. If Mr. Corrigan saw a view he liked, he'd find a way to film a scene in front of it, even if that meant paying people to use their property. Frank said he liked to pick the location first and then make up a story to go with it.

"They're all one-reelers," Frank explained—then overexplained. "Each story takes up one reel of film.

But Corrigan says he has ideas for longer pictures—two-reelers or even more. Stories told over two reels of film, you understand. Why, he's just brimming with ideas, Pearl—seems like he never runs out of new stories to tell."

Even though I squirmed at Frank's condescending tone—not to mention the familiar, and to my ears disrespectful, way he dropped the *Mr.* from Mr. Corrigan's name—I loved the way Frank's eyes went glittery when he was enthusiastic about a topic. I could tell he was brimming with plenty of ideas of his own. When he talked about *Mr.* Corrigan and making pictures, it was hard to imagine him going back to a humdrum life of riding fences and roping cattle.

⌘

"Bill said we'd find them here," Papa told me, steering his horse off the main road down a rutted path that led to the Cooper house. We knew Mr. and Mrs. Cooper from church. I'd been to their house once when Mama sent me to deliver some tomato starts to Mrs. Cooper. She'd brought me into her little kitchen and given me two big fresh-cooked doughnuts still warm from the kettle of oil she'd fried them in. Her house was tiny compared to ours, with thin wooden walls instead of thick stucco. It sat at the end of a lonely path that dipped down a hill, with a big mesa rising behind it.

My brothers, decked out like they were fixing to drive a herd to the stockyards for slaughter, were standing in front of the house in a group of other cowboys and a man wearing a farmer's chore clothes and a flat-topped hat. To my surprise I realized the farmer was none other than Bart, the evil cowboy from the week before!

Mr. Corrigan was huddled with the cowboys and the farmer man, talking a mile a minute. Nearby, Nell, the young lady with all the ringlets, stood cooling herself with a Chinese fan. She looked hot today and a bit cross. An older lady joined her and offered her a tin cup of something. Nell gave her a grateful smile and drank deeply. I swallowed, suddenly aware of the heat and wishing I had a cup of water myself.

There was a flurry of activity in front of the house. My brothers and the other cowboys moved off to the side of the house, near the kitchen garden.

"Take a couple of steps back," called Mr. Corrigan. "We're catching your shadows."

"Watch out for my cabbages!" called Mrs. Cooper

in an anxious voice. I hadn't noticed she was standing near the clump of people around the camera. She fixed Mr. Corrigan with a fretful glare. "I won't have them trampling my garden."

"We'll take care, won't we, lads?" said Mr. Corrigan soothingly. "All right, Nell, step into the house. On my call, come out and sweep the porch steps, and give us a nice dreamy face, full to the camera. Stop on this mark"—he pointed at the ground just in front of the steps—"and maybe lean on your broom a little. You're troubled by your father's determination to marry you off. You're so deep in your thoughts you don't hear the kidnappers sneaking up behind you." He turned to the cowboy cluster. "Kidnappers—got your marks?"

"Yes, sir," answered Ike.

"All right, then. Camera!" bellowed Mr. Corrigan. The camera operator began turning his crank.

"Action!" yelled Mr. Corrigan. The house door opened and Nell came down the steps with her broom. She gave it a few listless strokes over the steps, looking straight ahead with a worried expression. I don't know how she knew where to stop, because she never glanced down, but somehow she stopped right where Mr. Corrigan had pointed and rested her chin on her hands on the tip of the broom. Her big eyes had that dark charcoal-pencil smudge around the lashes again. The sun made a fluffy halo of her hair. She gave a sorrowful sigh, staring ahead toward the camera.

"Kidnappers, go!" called Mr. Corrigan. The bunch of cowboys, led by my brother Ike, began to tiptoe toward Nell. They crept up behind her, making an awful ruckus, but she didn't seem to notice. The biggest cowboy grabbed her by the waist and she screamed and kicked her legs. Bill tied a kerchief over her face. I knew it was make-believe but it was frightening to watch, and I found myself reaching over to clutch Papa's hand. Mr. Corrigan was calling out encouragement to the actors. Three or four of the cowboys lifted Nell and carried her away.

"Cut!" yelled Mr. Corrigan. The cowboys set Nell down and she raised the flap of the kerchief so she could see. Mr. Corrigan was conferring with the man behind the camera. Frank saw Papa and me watching and gave us an enthusiastic wave. This caught Nell's eye and she smiled in my direction. A second ago she had been shrieking with terror—it sounded so real, I'd been really afraid for her—but now she was laughing with the cowboys, calm and merry. It was all a big lark.

"All right, that's it for the house," said Mr. Corrigan. "Let's set up for the barn shots."

⌒

Papa and I weren't the only ones who started showing up to watch the filming, especially when it happened in town. The next time they shot a scene on Straight Street—Mr. Corrigan wanted the livery stable in the background, Frank said—the crowd of gawkers was so big that Mr. Corrigan had to shout into his megaphone to make everyone move out of range of the camera's round eye. The crowd scattered like minnows when you throw a rock into the creek, and then it re-formed itself behind the camera operator's back, where Papa and I had learned to stand.

I saw Walter Murray and Mary Mason and some other kids from school in the crowd. Walter was a good egg, the kind of kid who shook your hand if you beat him at a footrace or skunked him in a spelling bee. Mary, though . . . somehow I never could seem to get past the front porch with Mary, as Grandma would say. I'd known her since the first grade, but she was a town girl and I was a ranch kid. We only ever saw each other at school, and even there we didn't talk much. At recess Mary sat in the courtyard with the other town girls, while I mostly hunted lizards or played games with the ranch kids. I didn't like sitting next to Mary because she always wrinkled her nose like she smelled something bad—when I know for a fact I don't smell like anything except soap and (if Papa lets me ride Apple to school) horses. Personally, I think the smell of horse is one of the best smells in the world. I don't mean their manure, although even that smells sort of homey and cheerful—just plain horse scent, a little like hay and a little like leather, and a little like fresh-turned earth on a hot summer day. It's the smell of my father and brothers coming in from a hard day's work, with hat lines pressed into their hair and dust on their boots.

I waved hello at Walter and let it spill over to Mary, a little, to be polite. But she didn't notice me at all; she was goggling at Nell, who on this day was playing the part of a rich young lady who'd been kidnapped by bad guys. Nell's long curls trailed out over her shoulders in perfect coils. Mary's hand went to her own hair and she started twirling her locks into spirals. They uncoiled as soon as she took her finger out. Mary's brow wrinkled up and her mouth went thin with concentration.

I studied her, wondering what she was pondering so hard. She must have felt my gaze, because she suddenly looked in my direction and caught me staring. She made a face at me as if to say, *What are* you *looking at?* I shrugged and looked quickly away. Prissy Mary Mason wasn't one-tenth as interesting to look at as the bustle of the Flying Q gang when they were getting ready to do a scene.

But after Mr. Corrigan called "Action!" and Nell went back to screaming and struggling at her bonds, Mary Mason drew my eye again. She was watching the scene with big round eyes and making funny little

jerking motions with her hands behind her back, tossing her head, opening and closing her mouth like a fish. I gaped at her, wondering if she was having a fit.

Then it struck me—she was copying Nell. Her fish mouth was a silent imitation of Nell screaming. I looked back and forth between them. Nell's arms were tied behind her back, and so were Mary's, only the rope was invisible. Nell looked directly at the camera and yelled, "Help!" and Mary's mouth opened in wordless echo. She was starring in her very own moving picture, a silent performance just like the real thing.

I had to stifle a snort. Imagine a kid like Mary Mason acting in the pictures—what a hoot!

Chapter 6

That summer I shot up two inches at least. Grandma, who did most of the sewing, lowered the hems on all my dresses twice and then declared she was done until I stopped gaining leg overnight. "I can't keep up with you, Pearl," she sighed. "Borrow some trousers from your brothers if you don't want to go around showing your knees."

Music to my ears. You can ride in a dress but it's not the most practical garment. Some women ride sidesaddle, with both legs on the same side of the horse. You risk your neck trying to do real jumps that way, and even a simple gallop can be treacherous—your bottom keeps wanting to slide right off the saddle. Your other option is to hike up your skirts so you can ride properly, with a leg squeezing each side of the horse. That's how I usually rode but it does mean showing your knees to the world, and a good bit of petticoat. Mama had tolerated it when I was a little kid, because she knew I was a lot safer with a foot in each stirrup. But I could tell from the way she eyed my bare knees that my hitch-up-the-skirt days were numbered. So I was thrilled when Grandma gave up on keeping me decently clothed and sent me to the boys' ragbag.

I rummaged through the basket of Frank's out-grown clothes and found a pair of pants he'd worn when he was twelve or thirteen. Only one knee hole, and I patched it myself. It wasn't the neatest stitching job, but I didn't want to risk taking it to Grandma and having her decide the pants were too tatty for a girl. They were worn buttery-soft in the seat because Frank spent most of his time on the back of a horse.

I would too, if I could get away with it. But by the time I've tended the ostriches and done my house chores, the sun is high and the heat is starting to rise up from the baked earth. It's hard to care about riding, or anything really, when the sun is baking you into a cracker.

At least—that goes for riding Apple. Dinah is another story. Dinah gallops so hard and fast that we make our own wind, and it's better than a dunking in the pond. So when, on a hot afternoon, Papa told me Dinah needed a good run, I had her saddled up before you could say Jack Robinson.

The boys were filming at the Sanchez ranch out near Carter's Bluff that day, and Papa said I could go watch as long as I didn't get in the way. He didn't have to tell me twice.

As usual, Dinah attempted to choose our direction. I know her tricks, though, and I yanked hard on the reins to set her lolloping toward the bluff. They were in the middle of filming a scene when we arrived; I could tell at a distance from the way Mr. Corrigan was pulling at his hair. Whenever the camera was rolling, his hands went to the top of his head and clutched big fistfuls of hair. If the scene went smoothly, the hands slid back down. But if he wasn't happy with how things went, he tugged at his hair until it stood out in spikes and waves all over. He never wore a hat, which was a source of endless discussion amongst my cowboy brothers. They couldn't understand how he could see anything at all, squinting in the sun, let alone see so sharply he could tell if an actor's eyebrows were showing surprise instead of suspicion.

All I could see was a bunch of cowhands tearing around on horseback like a rodeo without a crowd. Mr. Corrigan was calling out instructions to them—"Now, Jack, you fire your gun at Ike. Ike, count to two and then slump over like you've been shot. It'd be swell if you could kinda hang off the saddle and let the horse run off with you. Think you can manage that?"

"Sure thing, Mr. C.," said Ike confidently.

It sounded simple enough to me but there was a whole bunch more talking and pointing, and a couple of practice runs for the actors to pace their horses from one mark on the ground to another, before they finally got down to filming the scene. I'd climbed down from Dinah to let her graze a bit in the field, where she wouldn't be in anybody's way, but when it sounded like Mr. Corrigan was ready to film the scene, I got back in the saddle. The pretend guns the fellas were using didn't fire as loudly as real ones, but they made a pretty sharp *pop* sound when the smoke came out—that's all it was, a pop and some smoke—and I was afraid Dinah might startle and bolt. I took a firm hold of the reins and kept my legs tight around her sides to let her know I was in charge for once. Anyway, I could see the action better from up there.

Everything went perfectly, at first. Mr. Corrigan called out instructions through his megaphone and the cowboys got into their starting positions. The costume lady had stuck a big black mustache on Ike. I had to shove my hand in my mouth to keep from guffawing. I thought he looked ridiculous but Mr. Corrigan seemed satisfied. He called out for the camera operator to start the film rolling. Then: "Action!" he cried, pointing at Ike.

Ike waved his gun around and Jack, the handsome bushy-haired actor, waved his gun back, and both of them hollered at each other but it was mostly nonsense. Didn't matter what they said, since no one would be hearing their words. Seemed like Ike was doing a lot of talking for someone who was only supposed to be a rider, but I'd noticed the distinction between actors and cowboys was getting a little blurry. Seemed like Mr. Corrigan kept wanting the bad guys in his stories to do a lot of fancy riding.

It was funny to think this rowdy, noisy scene would flicker in silence when people finally got to watch it. I hoped I would be one of them. Surely, Mama and Papa would take us all to see it in town when the picture was finished. Frank had explained that Mr. Corrigan had to send the film back east to be developed, and then someone would give it a bath in special chemicals that made the pictures appear, then cut it into pieces and stitch them back together and put in a bunch of writing to show what the actors were saying. I hoped whoever did that part was a person with a good imagination, because it seemed like he'd have to invent a whole lot of conversation. He certainly couldn't write down what Ike and the others were yelling today, which was mostly a loud description of what they were doing to each other.

"I'm gonna shoot you right through the heart!" yelled Ike, pointing his gun at Jack.

"Not if I shoot you first!" hollered Jack, aiming back.

Mr. Corrigan shouted, "Now!" and Jack pulled the trigger on his pretend gun. It popped even louder than I was expecting and a big cloud of smoke puffed out of the barrel. "One, *two*!" called Mr. Corrigan, and Ike jerked back like he'd been hit, and then he dropped his gun, clutched his chest, moaning, and slumped over, emitting a fearful death gurgle.

"What a ham," muttered the camera operator.

"It'll play well," Mr. Corrigan said, grinning beneath his mustache. "Kid's giving our Jack a run for his money."

I'd been right about the gun pops spooking Dinah. She reared her head back and rolled her eyes, but I kept a tight hold on the reins and she stayed put.

At least—until the real action began.

Chapter 7

Jack-the-hero had shot about half the bad-guy cowboys (including all three of my brothers), and his trusty deputy, Fred, had shot most of the others when all of a sudden another shot rang out, more distant but somehow more piercing than the others. Its crack startled Dinah something fierce. She reared up on her hind legs and almost dumped me to the ground. I clung tight, burying my fists in her mane, clutching the reins as hard as I could.

"Easy, girl, easy," I yelped, aiming for her ears but mostly talking straight into her neck. For a second all I could see was horsehair, but around me I heard a commotion of shouts and cries.

"Where'd it come from?" someone yelled. "Durn near took the skin off my nose!"

"Don't shoot!" screeched another voice. And yet another voice was hollering a stream of words that would make my mama wash out my ears if she knew I'd heard them—even worse than *durn*.

Suddenly Mr. Corrigan's voice bellowed out through the megaphone: "HOLD YOUR FIRE, YOU BLOOMING IDIOT! WE'RE FILMING A MOVING PICTURE!"

Well, that did it. The gunshots, the commotion, the megaphone blast echoing off the bluff—Dinah had had enough. She reared up again and this time my legs lost their hold. My lower half went flying free and when she came back down on her front hooves, both my legs wound up dangling on one side, free of the saddle and stirrups. My fists were still clenched in her mane and I was hanging there like a fish on a hook. The moment her hooves touched the ground, she tore off at a gallop with me hanging on for dear life.

Chapter 8

I think there was a lot more shouting but I couldn't hear much of anything over the pounding in my ears. My heart was hammering like a woodpecker. Dinah raced at full gallop, flying over tumbleweeds and sage bushes, with me flailing off to one side of her.

I was pretty scared, I'm not ashamed to admit. I knew how to fall off a horse—Papa had seen to that—but I didn't much fancy the notion of being shot off one at this speed, like a pebble flying off a slingshot. I was pretty sure my bones weren't as hard as pebbles.

So I did the only thing I could do—I hung on tight and tried to get my right leg up onto Dinah's back. It all happened a lot faster than I can tell it. I was too scared to speak, so I couldn't whisper gentling words into Dinah's pricked-back ears. I dug into either side of her neck with my elbows and hoped she'd get tired of running soon.

My right foot smacked the top of a bush and I nearly flew the rest of the way off. But the motion seemed to check Dinah just a little. Her pace slowed a fraction and I managed to dig my toes into her flank. I shoved hard against my heel and felt myself shift upward just enough to get my foot around her side.

As soon as my leg was over the side, I squeezed with all my might and wrenched myself up off Dinah's neck. I clutched at the reins, almost dropping

them as I unclenched my fingers from her mane. My palms were slick with sweat and at first the reins slid right through, which seemed to encourage Dinah into another burst of speed. But she was sweating too and I knew she was tiring. I yanked on the reins and finally found my voice.

"EASY, girl!" I screeched, before remembering that a screech was the opposite of how you wanted to calm a horse. "Easy," I repeated, softer this time, leaning close so she could feel my breath in her ear. Her eyes rolled back toward me. I felt her check just the tiniest bit.

Gradually, gently, I increased pressure on the reins, murmuring sweet nothings to Dinah all the while. And ever so gradually she began to slow down from a gallop to a jog. I patted her neck and tugged a big harder.

"Whoa, there," I said, and finally she stopped, breathing hard and flicking her ears angrily. "Whoa." My arms felt like noodles. I slumped down to rest my head on her neck. I could hear her heart pounding in rapid counterpoint to mine.

"Durn," I whispered into her mane, because nobody could hear me except my horse, and *she* wasn't likely to wash my mouth out with soap for swearing.

Chapter 9

It was a good thing Dinah was so worn out, because such an almighty ruckus was made by my brothers and the rest of the actors thundering up on their own horses that my poor old girl almost took off running again. I held her tight, and I think she must have recognized the scent or sound of my brothers' mounts, her stablemates. She made one little goatlike skitter and then stopped again, hanging her head, breathing hard.

"Pearl!" roared Ike, tearing up beside us. He always could outride the rest. His fake mustache was dangling by one corner, half in his mouth.

"Jiminy, Pearl. You all right?"

"Yeah," I said. It came out as a kind of squeak. My

stomach was wheeling with jittery butterflies and my head didn't feel too steady either. But I didn't want to look like a baby, so I gulped a breath and sat up straight and said as breezily as I could, "Sure, I'm the bee's knees."

Ike's mouth dropped open and his mustache fell the rest of the way inside. He sputtered and spat it into his hand, flicking his tongue like a barn cat working up a hairball.

"Well, I'll be du—" he said, cutting off short. That did it. I burst out laughing just as the rest of the company came barreling to a halt beside us.

Frank was an echo of Ike: "You all right, Pearl? Pearl, are you all right?" Bill didn't say a word; he just looked me up and down, checking to make sure I had all my limbs, I guess, and then slumped on his horse with his face in his hands.

I was surprised to see Mr. Corrigan was amongst the riders. He came up last, on the actor Jack's horse. I blinked at him in surprise.

"Well, I'll be," he murmured. "Here's the little lady, sitting there just as cool as a cucumber. I gotta say, kiddie, you must be the nerviest girl in the world."

"Oh, no, I'm terrified of caterpillars," I burst out before I knew I was going to say anything at all.

There was a startled silence and then suddenly all of them were roaring with laughter. Ike shot me a rueful look. Dinah whipped her head around with a furious glare, as if to say, *Can't you see I've had enough?*

"Easy, girl," I told her, hoping my voice didn't sound as shaky as it felt. The nerviest girl in the world wouldn't be shaky. I aimed for nonchalance. "What happened, anyway? Something spooked her awfully bad."

"We almost had us a real gunfight, is what," said Ike. He still had mustache hairs stuck to his lips. "You know Mr. Galloway? Rancher over yonder?" He pointed off toward the east.

"Yeah?"

"The fool thought we were real horse thieves," said Amos, the oldest cowboy in the Flying Q acting company. "Thought we were stealing Sanchez's stock."

"I can't blame him for misunderstanding what he saw, but coming in gun a-blazing—that's the foolish part," said Mr. Corrigan. "Even if you had been horse thieves, he might've shot one of the family, for all he knew."

"You mean some of those pops were real bullets?"

I yelped. I looked from Ike to Bill to Frank, my mouth wide enough to swallow my own mustache if I'd had one. "You coulda been shot!"

"And you could've broken your neck," said Frank in kind of a pale voice. "Jiminy, Pearl. That's the scaredest I've ever been in my life."

"That makes two of us," said Mr. Corrigan.

"That makes a *posse* of us," said Ike. And then the most surprising thing of the whole day happened. My big bold brother began to cry. He tried to cover it up by acting like he was wiping sweat from his brow, but I know what I saw. As we rode slowly back toward Carter's Bluff, I swear I saw him wipe tears from his eyes with his fake mustache.

Chapter 10

When we got back, the rest of the crew came rushing up to meet us.

"The little girl's all right?" asked the cameraman. He had his cap between his hands, mushed practically into a ball.

"Sure!" I said, spurring Dinah forward a little. She nickered at me grumpily. She was done with speed for the day.

The cameraman—his name was Mr. Gordon, but everyone called him Gordy—put a hand to his chest and breathed a huge sigh. "Thank all the saints and angels," he said. "I'm that glad to know it. I'd never have forgiven myself if—"

"What do you mean?" said Mr. Corrigan. "It was gunshots that spooked the horse. Nothing you did."

"I don't mean that," said Gordy, and his whole face turned the color of a ripe plum. He shot a sheepish look at the moving picture camera.

"You don't mean to say . . . ," began Mr. Corrigan, eyeing him shrewdly.

"Pure instinct, I swear it," said Gordy.

"What are you talking about?" asked Bill, looking perplexed.

"When the horse took off—" Gordy began, but he broke off, studying his feet.

"You filmed it," said Mr. Corrigan.

Gordy squared his shoulders and met Mr. Corrigan's eye. "That I did. And I understand if you want to sack me."

"Sack you? Why, man, I could kiss you!" Mr. Corrigan clapped him on the back, his eyes gleaming above a canyon-wide smile. "I mean"—and he turned back to me—"seeing as Pearl here came to no harm."

He dismounted his horse and turned to offer me a hand down from mine, but I was already sliding to the ground. I put a hand on the saddle knob in case my legs went to jelly. They felt a bit noodly but I kept to my feet.

"You filmed me?" I asked, feeling suddenly very shy.

"I did, lass," said Gordy. "I didn't think. I had my eye to the eyepiece and you were perfectly in frame. It was the most natural thing in the world to keep turning that crank."

"Do you think," said Mr. Corrigan, shifting his feet like a nervous horse, "you got it?"

Gordy grinned. "Oh, I got it, all right," he said. "At least, I kept rolling as far as I could see her. We'll have to see what it looks like. Might be nothing but a blur. That horse was running like the banshees were after her. And this little lass flapping like a rag doll in a gale." He shuddered and ran a hand over his eyes.

"How many minutes left on this reel?" asked Mr. Corrigan.

Gordy shrugged. "About six, I'd hazard."

Mr. Corrigan stroked his mustache. "We'll finish this story, then. But first I think we could all use a bit of dinner. Boys, water your horses and have some grub."

I felt a stab of guilt. The staggering discovery that

the camera operator had recorded my perilous flight had completely driven my poor horse out of my head. Poor Dinah, standing there with her head low and sides still heaving.

"I'll see to her," said Ike kindly.

"No, I will," said Frank. Bill was already reaching for the reins.

"No, I'll take care of her," I said. "She's my responsibility. Come on, girl."

I guided her to the water trough in the Sanchez pasture. Dinah rolled an eye to glare at me. I was probably going to have to walk the whole way home. But I didn't mind. I figured maybe that would give my heart time to quit galloping. I wasn't sure, anymore, whether it was racing because of the runaway or because Gordy had made a film of it.

Chapter 11

I couldn't stay to watch them film the rest of the story. By the time I got Dinah back home, which took halfway to forever, as I'd predicted, I was late for my afternoon chores. Papa scolded me on my way to the stable, Mama scolded me on my way to the kitchen, and Grandma scolded me on my way to the pie shelf in the pantry. (But then she cut me a big piece of dried-apple pie.)

Even the ostriches scolded me, when I finally made my way to their pen. Ostriches scold worse than all your parents and grandparents put together. The difference is, they'll scold you just for being alive—it doesn't particularly have much to do with your behavior. Unless you're late with their feed, and then watch out.

Today (since I really was late with their feed) I was prepared for their flappy, jabbery onslaught. I'd armed myself with a basketful of oranges. Not to throw at them, although sometimes the thought was tempting—just to shut them up.

Ostriches love oranges and they're so greedy they'll just gulp them down whole. It's the funniest thing you ever saw—a big round lump sliding slowly down the skinny stovepipe of an ostrich's throat. Papa calls it a party trick; whenever we have visitors, he tucks a couple of oranges in his pocket on the way to the ostrich pen, because it's so funny to watch folks gawk at the spectacle. You'd think the stupid birds would choke, but they're way too stubborn for that. They'd never give you the satisfaction.

I watched the orange lumps roll down the neck pipes and pondered my big adventure that day. Had Gordy really made a moving picture of me and my runaway horse?

I couldn't really imagine what it would look

like. Never mind the pictures—I'd never even seen a play, unless you counted the Nativity play at Christmas. Not a real play at one of the San Diego playhouses. My parents went, now and then, and they'd even been to the big opera house with (so I'd heard) real red velvet curtains and plush seats. Mama said the opera was sublime, and Papa said it was about what you'd get if you put some fancy ladies' gowns on our ostriches and watched them strut around, gabbling.

"Except our birds could probably stay on key better," he'd added.

"Oh hush, you," Mama had fussed. But she had laughed the way she always laughs when Papa pokes fun at something.

I wandered back to the kitchen, where Mama and Grandma were both flying around getting supper together.

"Can I go see the boys' movie when it plays?" I asked. I made an abrupt decision not to mention my own spell in front of the camera.

"Moo-vie?" asked Grandma, raising an eyebrow.

"Sure," I said. "It's a nickname for moving pictures. Everyone says it." I had a sudden rush of fear that *movie* was a naughty word like *durn* and I just didn't know it. But Grandma rolled her eyes and went back to slicing tomatoes.

"I'll never understand the fad for shortening perfectly good words," she said amiably. "Are you really so pressed for time that you can't choke out two more syllables?"

"Can't say I've ever noticed Pearl running out of time for any amount of words," teased Mama. I started to argue but remembered I was asking for something and had better be extra sweet.

"Can I, though? Go to the moving picture show?" I pronounced the phrase as slowly and elegantly as I could. Grandma snorted and flicked a last tomato slice onto its platter.

Mama sighed. "We'll have to see, Pearl. I don't know if those are fit places to take a child."

"Aw, Ike says it's just a bunch of chairs in a storefront, Mama. They hang up a sheet or screen and project the picture onto it." I didn't have the faintest idea what any of that meant, but I figured it sounded harmless enough.

"Hmm," said Mama, crinkling her brow. I knew right away that meant I wasn't going to get a *yes* out of her for now, and I didn't want to hang around for a *no*.

"I'd better get the table set," I said, reaching for a stack of plates. Mama eyed me knowingly, but I scooted out of the kitchen before she could say anything. Best leave it alone for a while, I decided. A watched egg never hatches, as Grandma says. (Which is silly, because I've watched eggs hatch loads of times.) I went slowly around the table, depositing a plate before each chair, trying to imagine what a moving picture would look like. Would a picture of my brothers really get up onto a screen somehow? Would they really be moving around up there, riding their horses across the stage?

Would *I*?

Chapter 12

When my mother heard about the pretend shoot-out that turned into a real shoot-out, she about had a fit. I couldn't tell who she was angrier at—the rancher with his hasty bullets or Mr. Corrigan for hiring my brothers in the first place. She even seemed a little mad at my brothers, although it wasn't their fault the rancher got confused and fired before he took a proper look around him.

"But, Ma—" Ike began, but she wasn't in the mood for discussion.

"Someone could have been killed," she said, her lips thin and tight. "It's the foolishest thing I've ever heard."

"No argument there," said Ike cheerfully. Bill shot

him a warning glance. Mama just glared at him and stalked off to pound some bread dough until it cried for mercy.

"Wish we hadn't finished that reel this afternoon," muttered Frank. "Then she'd have to let us go back."

"She can't stop me, anyway," said Bill. "I'm a grown man."

"You are not," scoffed Frank. "You're not of age for two more years."

"Nineteen is grown," Bill argued. "Papa was nineteen when he married."

"Good lord," said Ike. "Married. You?"

"Aw, hold your horses," said Bill. "I got no marrying plans anytime soon."

At any other time, I would have been absolutely riveted by this conversation—it had never occurred to me my brothers would one day marry and leave home, let alone that Bill was old enough to do it right this minute—but today all I could think of was what would happen when Mama found out about Dinah's run.

My first impulse was to beg my brothers not to tell But I knew Mama would be ten times angrier if she found out from someone else and I'd kept it secret. And I had no doubt she'd hear about it sooner or later. News traveled like wildfire in Lemon Springs.

I took a breath and marched into the kitchen.

I probably don't need to tell you what happened when I broke the news. Let's just say I'm pretty sure I know, now, what ostriches singing opera would sound like.

Chapter 13

I thought for sure that was the end of my watching my brothers make pictures. But I hadn't reckoned on Mr. Corrigan—none of us had.

"That man," my grandmother declared, "could sell saltwater to a sailor."

What happened is: He came home with my brothers after a day's filming. He brought a box of candy for my mother, the biggest one you can buy at the drugstore in Lemon Springs. She eyed it suspiciously and Mr. Corrigan even more so.

"I expect you've heard," he said coolly, "about your Pearl's little adventure the other day." He winked at me.

I thanked my lucky stars I'd spilled the beans to Mama right away.

"Indeed I have," said Mama, unbending not one inch. She hadn't so much as glanced at the box of chocolates he had thrust into her hands.

"She's quite a rider," said Mr. Corrigan.

Mama's chin tilted and her hands tightened on the chocolate box, like she was squaring up for a fight.

"Good thing," she said.

Mr. Corrigan nodded companionably.

"I need a girl like Pearl for my next picture," he said. "It's just a little part. She runs out of a house, sees her mama in danger, and rides a horse to get help."

"You don't have any girls in your troupe?" Mama asked suspiciously.

"Nope. There was a vaudeville family—ma, pa, three kids—who made a couple of pictures with us in Chicago before we came west. But they missed the singing. Had some real fine singing voices, they did. They felt like they were wasting their talents in moving pictures. Nobody to hear them sing, you know."

Mama's nails tapped on the box of candy. "Hmm."

Now, this was surprising. The second Mr. Corrigan had said he needed a "girl like Pearl" for a picture, I had fully expected Mama to shoo him away like a stray dog. But *hmm* wasn't her shooing noise. It was her thinking-something-over noise.

"We pay handsomely," Mr. Corrigan added.

"Hmm," said Mama.

"How handsomely?" said Grandma, making us all jump. She was standing in the doorway of the kitchen with a mixing bowl propped on her hip. She must have been listening the whole time.

"Half what I'm paying your sons," said Mr. Corrigan. "That's the usual rate for a child. It'll be two days' work and I'd see to it she's home in time for chores."

He shot me a glance that was like a wink without the wink. A twinkly kind of look. I found I was holding my breath.

"Hmm," said Mama. "I'll need to speak to my husband."

My breath rushed out hard. I knew what that meant. I was going to make a picture.

It wasn't until later that I realized how clever Mr. Corrigan had been. Instead of telling my mother his man had filmed me on the runaway horse, which would probably have made her see red, he had (apparently) thought up a whole new story that would use that other piece of film. Hadn't he said something about needing me to ride a horse to get help?

Chapter 14

"What we need," said Mr. Corrigan, running his hands through his hair, "is a shot of the horse running away while you cling with all your might. Just like the other day, only you'll have a good seat instead of hanging on by your fingertips. It has to feel dangerous, like any second you might fall and be trampled to bits. Do you think you could manage it? I don't want to put you in real danger."

"I don't see where the danger is," I said, puzzled. "You just want me to ride at a gallop and pretend I'm scared?" I knew it wouldn't be like the other time, because I'd be in control of my horse. And like he said, sitting properly in the saddle.

"Er, I guess that's right," said Mr. Corrigan, breaking into a grin. "I know you can manage the riding part. But I'll need your face toward the camera, and you've got to look utterly petrified. It's a lot to think about, and that's going to pull your attention away from managing the horse, you know."

I chewed my lip, thinking it over. The acting part did make me nervous. What if I did it wrong? Looked silly? There was more anxiety in that notion than in the idea of riding a runaway horse. What if I looked ridiculous and everyone laughed, and Mr. Corrigan was disappointed in me?

"That's it!" cried Mr. Corrigan. "That's just what I'm looking for. Absolute terror. You're a natural, kid. Think you can do that at racing speed?"

It turns out acting is harder than it looks. For weeks I'd been watching my brothers and the Flying Q acting company strut around making big faces and mouthing things at the camera. But Mr. Corrigan seemed dissatisfied with my big faces. His voice sounded calm but his hands buried themselves in his hair, ruffling it up in spikes.

"Honey, you look like you ate a peck of green apples. Can you show me scared instead of stomach-ache-y?"

We were practicing without the camera, since film was so costly and Mr. Corrigan couldn't afford to waste it on stomachache faces. He kept having me ride the horse along a path with my head turned to the side, staring at the blank black face of the camera box as we galloped past, over and over. But Gordy hadn't put the gizmo in motion yet.

"Tell you what. Don't try to look scared. Just open your eyes real big and stare hard like you see a twister coming in the distance."

I trotted the horse back to the starting point and turned her around to try again. Gordy gave me an encouraging wave. It felt ridiculous to turn my head sideways instead of looking at our path ahead. Who rode looking sideways?

Then I noticed the small crowd gathered in the watching places back behind the camera and to the sides. It was kids from town mostly. Walter Murray, the James brothers—and Mary Mason. And she looked furious. She was glaring right at me like I'd just kicked her in the shins or something. My eyes widened.

"That's it!" yelled Mr. Corrigan. "Now ride!"

I kicked Dinah's flanks and she leapt forward in her usual urgent way. But I barely paid attention this time to where she was going because I couldn't pull my eyes away from the force of Mary Mason's livid stare. If her eyes had been hornets, they'd have stung me.

"Perfect!" cried Mr. Corrigan. We were at the far end of the path now, and Dinah turned around and trotted back toward the starting mark without my asking. Mr. Corrigan came up alongside us, chuckling.

"That horse is better trained than half my company," he said. "Say, kid, that was swell. Just what we want. Think you can do it again with the camera rolling?"

I shrugged. I really had no idea. I glanced back at Mary Mason and she was *still* watching me like a very hungry hawk eyeing a nice fat mouse. I noticed her hair was curled today in long ringlets cascading over her shoulders, like Nell's.

I couldn't help it—I stuck my tongue out at her. Now her eyes went wide and her hands flew to her hips. Then she wheeled around and turned her back to me.

"Friend of yours?" said Mr. Corrigan wryly. He was looking from Mary to me with a smile quirking the corner of his mouth. "Cute kid."

My breath came out hard through my nostrils like I was an irritated horse. Dinah answered with a chummy whicker.

"Ready?" said Mr. Corrigan. "Let's go, then. This one counts."

He barked some instructions through his megaphone—taking care to aim it well away from Dinah's sensitive ears—and the crew sprang into motion. Gordy lowered his eye to the camera's eyepiece, and Mr. Corrigan's spectacled assistant scolded everyone to keep back out of view.

I gave Dinah an absent pat on the neck, scanning the huddle of onlookers for Mary Mason's angry face. She still had her back to me but I swear she could tell I was looking at her, because she glanced over her shoulder, and mouthed, with her snooty chin high in the air, *Pooh*. At least, I don't think she said it out loud. But I could read it just as clear as if she'd spoken the word—like she was starring in a moving picture of her own.

Then she stalked away down the street without a backward glance.

"What's eating her?" I murmured to Dinah, but Dinah didn't know either. And suddenly I realized that even though Mary had marched her evil glare away, everyone else's eyes were on me. A jolt of panic struck me like lightning.

"Camera!"

Gordy starting cranking. I tried to put Mary out of my mind.

"Action!" cried Mr. Corrigan. Dinah didn't even wait for my kick this time; she just took off like a wolf was at her heels. Or maybe Mary Mason.

I didn't have time to think about anything. I

just hung on tight, kept my face aimed at the top of Gordy's head above the camera box, and prayed I wouldn't make a fool of myself in front of all those people.

"Cut!" hollered Mr. Corrigan as Dinah reached the far mark. "Get it?" he called to Gordy.

"Got it," said Gordy.

"Good."

And that was how I made my first on-purpose scene in a moving picture.

Chapter 15

Ike was happiest when Mr. Corrigan asked him to do some crazy stunt like fall off his horse or pretend to get dragged along behind it with one foot in the stirrup. (Personally, I couldn't see how *pretending to get dragged* was any different from actually getting dragged, except that the path had been swept smooth and soft, with all the bigger rocks carted away so Ike wouldn't clonk his head.)

But Frank seemed to think Mr. Corrigan had the more exciting job. He peppered him with questions about how the camera film would get turned into a moving picture, and who came up with the story ideas. Mr. Corrigan said that when the studio started back east, his bosses at Flying Q would buy stories from any old writer at twenty-five dollars each, which struck me (and Frank) as a pretty impressive wage. But once they sent him out west—"because of the patents men, you know," Frank told me—he got tired of waiting for scripts to show up in the mail, so he started thinking up his own.

"I don't know," I told Frank.

"Don't know what?"

"About the patents men. Who are they?"

Frank rolled his eyes at my ignorance, but he always liked a chance to lecture. It seemed there was a man back east, a very rich, important man named Thomas Edison. He was an extremely clever man with many useful inventions to his credit, such as the phonograph and the electric lightbulb. And he was one of the people who figured out how to build motion picture cameras.

"Is he a magician?" I said wonderingly.

"No. But as smart as one. And he's a shrewd businessman, too—maybe a little too shrewd, is the problem. He buys up patents to things and then he owns the ideas behind the things, and people have to pay him to use the ideas."

"Patents? Like patent leather shoes?"

Frank chuckled. "Naw. A patent is a piece of paper

you get from the government that says you own the idea behind an invention and you're the only person who gets to use the idea. Edison has a heap of patents from his own inventions, but he's so rich he also buys 'em from other inventors and then he just gets richer."

I wasn't sure I understood, but I didn't want Frank to think I was a baby, so I nodded as wisely as I could. It's maddening when the person who knows a thing you want to know treats you like you're a ninny for not knowing it already. Somehow, it seemed like Frank was always that person.

"Well, anyway, he bought the patent to an important component of motion picture cameras. It's called the Latham Loop and it keeps the film from getting tangled up inside. And now Mr. Edison says anytime someone uses a camera with a Latham Loop, they owe him money. And if you won't pay up, he sends his men to make you."

That sounded unnerving. "Like . . . henchmen? Are they mean?"

"Sometimes. Sometimes they shoot your camera to bits so you can't use it at all!"

"But that's awful!" I cried.

Frank shrugged. "That's why Flying Q came to Lemon Springs, you know," he said. "To—"

"To escape from the henchmen!"

Frank laughed. "Something like that. California is too far away for Edison to bother about. At least, that's what the film company is hoping!"

"But couldn't the henchmen take a train?"

Frank hooted scornfully. "Don't be a worrywart, Pearl. No one's coming to shoot Mr. Corrigan's camera. Besides, how would they even know where to look? I bet those Easterners have never even heard of Lemon Springs. It's not exactly a bustling metropolis."

I started to ask what a metropolis was but I couldn't stand to sound ignorant about one more thing. I wished Frank would explain things without being so lordly about it. It seemed like there was a lot more to making a picture than riding a horse or waving your arms around.

Chapter 16

Mr. Corrigan hadn't mentioned I would have to act in other parts of the movie. I thought it was just the runaway-horse bit. But of course you couldn't make a whole picture out of a girl on a horse. Mr. Corrigan said we had to show how the girl wound up on the horse.

"But that part would come first," I said, confused.

"Oh, that doesn't matter. We're going to cut up the film and stitch it back together in the right order."

"Why not just film it in the right order in the first place?" I asked.

"Gotta cut it up anyway to put in the title cards," he explained. Those were cards with words printed on them so the audience could read what the characters were saying.

So the next day I came back with my brothers, wearing the same plaid dress as the day before. We were back at the Cooper farm, because Mr. Corrigan liked the big front porch with its three steps down to the ground.

"Pearl, you're going to stand in the house where no one can see you, just beside the door. You'll hear a squabble on the porch and you're going to walk out right in the middle of it. I'll let you know when to come. Stop in the doorway for a minute, forward so you aren't in shadow, and you're going to see Nell— she's your ma—in an argument with Bart. He's the villain."

"He's always the villain," I said.

"I reckon he's just got that kind of face," said Mr. Corrigan.

Bart winked at me. It didn't look a bit villainous at the moment, but I remembered how scary he had looked that time he was holding Nell captive on his horse.

"You just stand there for a second and watch them squabble," Mr. Corrigan went on. "Bart won't notice you're there, see, but Nell will. She'll tell you to go for help, and then I want you to nod *yes ma'am* at her and run off the porch in that direction." He pointed toward the barnyard. "Then you just stay put. Don't let Bart see you go. Got it?"

"I think so," I said, feeling jittery as a grasshopper. I wished I could stick to riding horses.

Mr. Corrigan made us practice it a couple of times. The first time, he burst out laughing when I stopped on my mark to watch the argument between Nell and Bart. It was a good fight, with lots of screaming, and I didn't mind watching it at all.

"You're supposed to look scared, honey!" laughed Mr. Corrigan. "Not excited, like you're at the races."

"Oh!" I said, surprised. "But it *is* exciting." I heard Gordy chuckle from his spot behind the camera.

"To you—Pearl," he said. "But you're not Pearl in this story. You're a scared little girl whose mama needs help. Look worried, like you did yesterday. Got it?"

I shrugged uncertainly. The story didn't make much sense to me. If it were my real mother needing help, I'd run up and kick the villain. But Mr. Corrigan was boss, so I tried it his way in the next practice run.

"Scareder," he called. "No, don't look at me; look at Nell. Clasp your hands or something."

I grabbed one hand with the other and wiggled my fists around.

Bart and Nell laughed. "You got a frog in there, kid?" Bart teased.

"Like this, honey," said Nell in her soft, kind voice. She clasped her hands together and held them in front of her heart. Her face crinkled up into an expression of terror. Then in a flash the scared look was gone and she was smiling at me again. "See?"

"How did you *do* that?" I breathed in wonder.

"Do what?"

"For a second there I thought you saw a ghost! It almost gave me the willies!"

Nell's pretty laugh rippled out. "Why, Pearl, honey, that's *acting*. You just think what it feels like to be in a moment—a scary one, a happy one, a brokenhearted one—and you let the feeling show on your face."

I hadn't had to rustle up a pretend-scared yesterday on the horse. I'd been plenty scared for real because of all the people watching me. And they were watching me today, but not as many—not Mary

Mason, for example. I'd have died before I admitted it to anyone else, but that mean look she gave me had really rattled me. And I guess it was the right kind of rattled to show on my face.

I wasn't rattled today. But I tried to make myself feel scared. I thought of the scariest thing I could come up with. A caterpillar. No, an army of caterpillars. Millions of them, falling out of trees into my hair and down the back of my dress.

"That's it!" cried Nell. "You've got it!"

"Why, you're a natural," said Bart.

After that, we practiced a few more times and I started to feel like I knew what I was doing. But right before we did it for real, with the film rolling, Nell said, "You don't want it to get too pat, like you know what's coming. Remember, you aren't Pearl who's practiced this a bunch of times; you're my little girl on our farm and this terrifying thing is happening to you for the very first time."

She said it in such a chilling voice that I got goose bumps. For just a flash it felt real. The goose-bumpy feeling was still on me when Mr. Corrigan yelled "Action!" and I felt almost shaky as I stood in the doorway watching my pretty young ma struggle with the evil robber who meant to do her harm. I found I was twisting a big wad of my pinafore up in my hands as I watched the struggle. Then Nell—Ma—screamed for me to go for help, and I bolted like a jackrabbit.

"Cut!" cried Mr. Corrigan, and I could tell from the way he smoothed his hair down that I'd done it just the way he wanted.

But it was the oddest thing. As soon as it was over, I really did feel shaky with fear. Was that how acting worked? You pretended so hard it became real?

Chapter 17

At the end of my two days' work, Mr. Corrigan paid me fifty cents—*fifty whole cents!*—and clapped me on the back like I was one of the cowboys. It seemed like a vast amount of money just for riding a horse, running off a porch, and one other scene where I ran up to a sheriff (it was Jack, of course, who always got the biggest good-guy part) and tugged on his sleeve, begging him to help my ma. After that, I wasn't in the story anymore. I didn't even know how it ended, because they filmed it on Feather Day.

Feather Day happens once a year, when Mama has collected enough ostrich feathers to make it worth a trip by train to the millinery district in the city. Riding a train is like riding Dinah, only you're inside its belly and it goes even faster. Except when it pokes along in and out of a station, which I guess is more like riding Apple than Dinah.

Mama washed and combed the feathers and put them carefully into two big canvas sacks. We held these carefully on our knees on the train, never letting go for a second. Mama was saving the feather money up to send Ike to college. She had tried to talk Bill into college but he said he was content to be a rancher. Ike used to talk about studying to be an engineer so he could build bridges and things, but that was before Mr. Corrigan came along. These days he and Frank both seemed a lot more interested in fake mustaches and cowboy pictures and motion picture cameras.

It made me feel queasy inside to think of my brothers going off to college or moving away from home. Who would wink at me across the table if Ike was gone? And Bill . . . he never said much but I always felt sort of safe and comfortable when Bill was around. He was like our bell post: steady and solid and ready for emergencies. Bill was the one we always hollered for when there was a rattler in the yard; he'd just stroll up with a shovel and take its head off without batting an eye. Once, when I was eight years old, I was hoisting an ostrich egg out of the hay, and not two feet away from me there was a big diamondback all coiled up and hissing. Bill heard me shriek and came running, and he leaned over the rail fence and lifted me out of the pen to safety, so gently the egg I was clutching didn't even crack. He sure did crack that rattlesnake in the head, though.

Even Frank. Sure, he annoyed me, acting all wise and superior like some kind of hoity-toity professor—but I couldn't picture our ranch without him. He acted like a know-it-all—but as far as I could tell, he kind of *did* know it all. Why else would I keep pestering him with questions even when he made me feel like an ignorant baby?

But thoughts of my brothers fell away behind me as the train chugged along the canyons and ridges toward the city. The wide, empty chaparral began to fill up with houses and farms, more and more the farther west we got. I wished I could ride up front with the engine driver, or better yet, right on top of the train, where I might get a view of the sea. Surely, someone could figure out how to put a kind of saddle on top of a train so you didn't have to waste the journey inside its metal belly. That Mr. Edison could probably figure it out, I supposed. But then he might send henchmen to make you pay extra to sit on it.

We passed the gleaming white walls of the mission tucked in its canyon and, not long after that, the old fort high on a hill with the same white stucco walls shining through the trees. I knew that meant we were getting close to the city. We took the train all the way to San Diego near the harbor, which is as far west as you can go. Any farther and you'd wind up in the Pacific Ocean.

From there we took a hack to the millinery shop. It was pulled by the laziest horse I ever saw, ten times pokier than Apple on her pokiest day. Automobiles kept whizzing past us, blaring their Klaxon horns—more autos than I'd ever seen in my life—a dozen at least, maybe more!

"My goodness," remarked Mama. "They're popping up like mushrooms, aren't they?"

"Can't we get an auto?" I pleaded, but I knew Mama would scoff at the notion. She said they were loud and smelly.

"So are ostriches," I pointed out.

"Don't be pert, Pearl."

I watched buildings slide slowly past the hack's

window and tried to decide what was smellier, an ostrich or an auto. Neither one could hold a candle to a horse, which had a nice earthy smell somewhere between hay and woodsmoke, and could take you flying across open country so fast you felt like a bird. A real bird, not a snippy, land-bound haystack like an ostrich.

The feathers were nice, though, I had to admit. Mama only took the best ones to the hatmaker's, and since the birds dropped all their feathers during molting season every year, I had as many as I wanted to play with. When I was little, I tried to stitch a bunch of them together to make myself wings, but Ike pointed out if ostriches couldn't use them to fly, why would it work for a person? Anyway, the feathers kept tickling my nose and making me sneeze.

Mama always did business with Mr. Abrams on Broadway. His office was in the back of a big open room where half a dozen girls sat at high tables, combing feathers and sewing them to hats. Mama strode straight through between the tables with our enormous sacks and disappeared into the little boxy office. I knew she'd be in there forever and a day, haggling over prices. Grown-ups' money talk was just about the most boring thing I could think of.

It was much more interesting in
the big feather room with little
specks and motes of fluff floating
in the air like dandelion seeds. A
bit sneezy, maybe, but a beautiful sight, especially in the shafts of
light angling through the high windows, which seemed to catch and
hold the fluff in a kind of suspen-
sion, like tiny tadpoles in a clear pool.

I always appreciated our birds more
here, surrounded by piles of ostrich feathers,
than I did when I was in their presence. It seemed to
me our feathers were much bigger and silkier than
the scores strewn on the tables around me. Our birds
were more richly colored, a gray so soft it was almost
blue in the right light, or creamy white like the inside
of an eggshell. It wasn't something you noticed when
the feathers were still attached to the birds, because
the birds' bad tempers ate up all your attention. If
you stopped to admire their colors, you might get
clouted on the head by a big hard beak that may as
well have been a piece of stovepipe. Some things,
like ostriches and brothers, were easier to appreciate
from a distance.

Chapter 18

All that summer the Flying Q crew filmed picture after picture—one a week, give or take. My brothers were in most of them, one way or another. They were ranchers and robbers and, once, Catholic priests at a mission church. Jack with the wavy hair was always the hero—a brave farmer defending his stock from cattle thieves, or a sheriff bringing outlaws to justice, or a young man pining for the love of his beautiful Nell. Nell's part always seemed the same—she was a girl in danger, sometimes resourceful and sometimes pretty helpless, and always rescued by Jack in the end. Sometimes I wondered if Mr. Corrigan had only known one girl in his whole life. Didn't he know we came in different varieties? Why, look at me and

Mary Mason—as different as Dinah and Apple, as different as ostriches and chickens.

I hung around the crew every chance I got, especially Gordy, in case Mr. Corrigan needed my help in another picture. But he didn't seem to come up with many stories involving kids. I didn't care too much, to be honest, because it had been pretty nerve-wracking to have Mary—to have all those people—watching me try to act scared.

But I loved the excitement of a shoot. That's what they called it when they filmed a scene. I liked the bustle, the noise, the way Mr. Corrigan's excitable hands made his hair stand up all spiky during the getting-ready parts. I liked the way he marched back and forth in his boots, hollering orders like an army captain. I liked the way Gordy slid his cap around backward when it was time for him to peer into his eyehole, and then slid it back brim-front during the waiting-around times.

Seemed like waiting around was one of the main jobs of anyone involved in making a picture. Waiting around while Mr. Corrigan explained to the actors what to do in their next scene. Waiting around for a cloud to pass or the wind to die down. Waiting around while Gordy fiddled with his camera lens or figured out where was the best place to stand the camera during a scene. Waiting around while Mr. Corrigan picked out the right size of megaphone for shouting his instructions through. He used a little one for close-in scenes and a big one for booming at the cowboys far across a field.

I didn't mind the waiting-around one bit because it often meant a chance to chat with Gordy. I liked his twinkly eyes and his light, lilting accent. He was born in Ireland, he told me, and came to America with his father when he was a lad, after his mother died.

"Sure and he couldn't bear to lay eyes on the lanes they'd walked together. He sold our cottage and our cow, and we sailed to Boston. And then it seemed even an ocean wasn't enough space between him and the memories that overpowered him with grief. He bought us a pair of train tickets and we came all the way west until we bumped into the next ocean. He set up a barbering shop in San Juan Capistrano, and that's where I did the rest of me growin' up. That's how I came to meet Mr. Corrigan and his acting troupe."

"Gordy, that's so sad! About your mother."

" 'Tis indeed, lass. But 'twas a long time ago. I was old enough when she died to remember her—and for that I'm forever grateful, for she was a grand woman, was Molly Gordon—but young enough for my heart to heal. It wasn't so for my poor father. He lived out his days with a hole in his chest where his heart used to be."

I loved Gordy's stories, even the sad ones. He was full of tales about the "little people" back in Ireland—he said it was a pity America didn't have anything of the kind, and he reckoned if there once had been fairy people here, they must have all disappeared under the hills when the white men came and snatched the lands away from the Indians. The little people despised land thieves, he told me. Most of the ones in Ireland had disappeared when the English took control of the land.

"Although they'll not hesitate to steal a babe out of its cradle if they've a grudge against its parents," he added. "They don't consider that stealin', exactly. More like getting their just deserts."

I shuddered at the thought. "Did you know any babies who were stolen?"

"Only one. It belonged to our neighbor down the road. At least, my mother said it must have been a changeling, the way it fussed and fretted all the livelong day."

"Suppose it just had colic?" I asked. At Mass on Sundays there were always a few mothers walking up and down the chapel side-aisles with their colicky babies. Our priest didn't mind if they drowned him out during the Latin parts of the Mass, but if a baby squawked during his homily, he furrowed his brow and glared at the poor mother until she ducked outside.

"But if you ask me," I explained to Gordy, "the babies are generally more interesting to listen to than the homily. My, how some of them can howl!"

Gordy's eyes crinkled into a laugh. He had amazingly laughing eyes, but the laughs that came out of his mouth were soft and short, often just one low, appreciative *Ha!*

"I take it you enjoy a good ruckus, Pearl?" he asked, twinkling.

"Oh yes!" I agreed. "The ruckus-ier, the better. That's why I like watching Mr. Corrigan direct. Even when he's not shouting, it seems like he's making a ruckus."

This time Gordy burst out with a real multisyllable laugh. He swiveled his cap brim to the back, and then swiveled it to the front again because it wasn't time to look in the eyehole, and then he whisked the cap off his head and dabbed his eyes with it.

"Ah, Pearl, you are a one," he said. "You must keep your mother on her toes."

"Oh, no, she's much taller than I am," I said. "Although I'm getting taller by the hour, according to my grandmother."

Just then Mr. Corrigan picked up his biggest megaphone, which meant the cowboys were about to ride. I stuck my fingers in my ears because, unlike the cowboys, I didn't have a whole field between me and Mr. Corrigan.

"Say, Pearl," murmured Gordy when the booming instructions died down. "How'd you like to turn the crank?"

"What?" I gasped, dumbfounded. "On the camera?"

"Heh," chuckled Gordy. "Sure and I don't see any automobiles around here to wind up, do you?"

"Oh, Gordy!" I cried. He found a crate for me to stand on and showed me what to do.

"The moment Mr. C. calls out 'Camera!' you want to start the crank turning and keep her going until he says 'Cut!' Got it?"

"Yes!" I said confidently. I'd watched Gordy at work umpteen times by now. He nodded and swiveled his cap backward, ready to peer into the eyehole.

I couldn't believe my luck. A couple of butterflies went zinging around in my stomach—suppose I did it wrong and ruined the shot?—but the only way to ruin it would be to stop turning the crank too soon. Wild horses couldn't keep me from turning that crank. Why, a rattlesnake could slither right over my foot and I wouldn't stop. A caterpillar could creep right up the back of my dress and—

I shuddered. All right, maybe one thing could cause me to abandon my post. But there were no trees overhead and no caterpillar-hunting brothers to hang off their branches even if there were any. All three of my brothers were across the field on their horses, ready to ride.

"Camera!" boomed Mr. Corrigan.

"Eek," I squealed, giving the crank a twist.

"That's it, nice and steady; keep your pace. She'll tell you how fast she wants to go."

The camera's a she? I wanted to ask but didn't dare risk breaking my concentration. I knew ships were called *she*, so maybe it applied to other inventions, too. Were trains *he* or *she*? What about telephones?

"Action!" barked the megaphone. The cowboys thundered toward us across the field and I cranked for all I was worth.

⁓

"You did what?" sputtered Frank at the supper table that night when I boasted about my tremendous accomplishment.

"I took some film!" I crowed. "Or, well, I helped, at least. Gordy was the one looking in the eyehole."

Frank opened his mouth to say something but snapped it shut. I could see that he was furious. He was jealous! Of me! His ignorant little sister! I wanted to gloat. I wanted to crow about my superior experience. I sat up straighter and taller and was about to speak when I felt Grandma's eyes on me. Her brows were raised a little, as if she was curious to see what would happen next. But I sensed it was a particular kind of curiosity. I felt suddenly as if I were about to take a test at school.

"Say, Frank," I said, trying to sound nonchalant. I was grateful for Nell's acting lessons because I didn't feel nonchalant at all. "Want me to ask Gordy to give you a try? I'm sure he'd say yes. He's ever so nice."

Frank's eyes lit up like he'd found a gold nugget in a hen's nest. "Do you think he would? Gee, Pearl, that'd be swell!"

Across the table Grandma smiled a very small smile and quietly slid the jam pot in my direction.

If there was a test, I think I passed.

Chapter 19

One day when I was hanging around the Flying Q folks as usual, Mr. Corrigan said he needed a sick child for a scene in a new picture they were filming the next day. "Think you can lie in bed and suffer into the camera?" he asked me.

"Suffer?"

"I want big sad eyes in a pale, sad face," he explained.

"On horseback again?" I asked hopefully.

He chuckled. "No, honey. In a sickbed. We're shooting indoors tomorrow morning. Ask your folks, all right? Same pay as before."

I raced home to ask. Mama said she didn't see that I could come to much harm lying in a bed, so why not. I could hardly sleep that night, I was so keyed up. Another picture!

Seemed like my ostrich chores took ten times as long as usual the next morning. I washed up as fast as I could and would have dashed out the door straight-away but Mama made me sit down at the breakfast table. Papa needed Apple and Dinah that day, so I had to ride behind Bill on his chestnut mare. I hated riding double, smushed up against my brother's back, unable to see what lay ahead. My neck got a crick from being turned to the side for too long, watching the scrubby bushes of the chaparral bounce past. It was too bad Gordy wasn't there with his camera be-cause I could have suffered into it for real.

The shoot was in town today, in a big old house near the post office. The first thing I discovered when we got there was that I wasn't the only kid playing a part in the story this time. Mary Mason, Walter Murray, and a couple of other town kids were there too, wearing raggedy old clothes the costume mistress had handed out. Mary's eyes went narrow and mean when she saw me. I glared right back at her. Two could play at that game.

"Oh good, here's Pearl," said Angela, the costume lady. "Go behind the sheet and change into this dress, honey." She thrust a wad of dingy brown fabric into my hands. "Boys, you run outside now and wait until you're called. I guess it don't matter if you get dirty, since you're supposed to look like pitiful little beggar children."

"Why are we living in such a fancy house if we're beggars?" I asked.

Mary snorted. "Shows what you know!" she said.

"What's eating you?" I fired back. It was really beginning to get my goat that she seemed so irked with me all the time. Sure, we'd never exactly been friends, but I didn't think we'd been the opposite of friends. We hadn't been *anything*, really. Before the pictures, Mary was just some kid at school, and not one of the really interesting ones like Joey Sanchez, who could walk on his hands, or Juniper Howard, who once rode a train all the way to Baltimore, Maryland, and back. I could remember a few times when Mary had recited for the class—she was pretty good at holding your interest; even the rowdy boys stopped socking each other's arms to listen to her—but apart from that, she didn't stand out in my mind much. She was a town girl in shiny shoes who didn't appreciate the smell of horse. Not much there to capture my attention.

But now she was a source of intense fascination, because however neutral I felt about her, she certainly seemed to have strong feelings about me, and none of them were complimentary, as far as I could tell.

She didn't answer, just rolled her eyes at me. Her hair was curled into sausage ringlets again. I don't know how her mother ever got anything else done—she must have had to spend hours a day on Mary's perfect hair and speckless clothes. Ugh. I'd rather clean the ostrich pen than sit in a chair for an hour while my mother wrapped my hair around hot irons.

Mr. Corrigan was in a hurry to film the scene while the light was right. Turned out we were shooting in an old shed out behind the fancy house. It had been fixed up—or maybe unfixed is more like it—to look like a run-down old shack. Against one bare board wall was a rickety bed with shabby covers made of old flour sacks. Mr. Corrigan told me to get into the bed and look deathly ill.

"Now, you just lie there, Pearl, and look out toward Gordy with big sad eyes. You're real sick. That's it. The rest of you kids just stand here against the wall and try to look hungry. No fidgeting, mind. You just watch while Nell acts her part."

It seems Nell was the mother of all the raggedy

children, including poor sick me. She looked kind of young to have so many kids, but what did I know. Mr. Corrigan talked her through her part. She was worried her little daughter—me—was going to die, and in this scene she was supposed to carry on for a bit and then send Jack out the door to fetch a doctor. I was supposed to lie still and pale in the bed and look like I might give up the ghost if he didn't get here soon. Easy enough.

The shed had two big doors that opened wide— wide enough to get a carriage through—and these were spread all the way open to let in as much light as possible. Gordy muttered and peered through the eyehole of his camera, and moved it a little this way and a little that way, and finally he said he was ready.

Everything would have been just fine if Mary hadn't snorted. I was suffering into the camera just like I was supposed to, and Nell cried and carried on like she had to shoot her favorite horse. She wrung up her apron between her fists and cried into it, and then raised her eyes to the heavens and implored God to save her precious girl, and tore around the room look-ing for something to pay the doctor with when he ar-rived. It was obvious I was her favorite kid, from the way she carried on. She smoothed my hair off my forehead and put a cool cloth on it like I had a fever. I knew fevers made people go out of their minds sometimes, seeing visions and things, and it sure seemed like this kid must be sick enough for visions, or her mama wouldn't be so distraught. So I stared up into the air like I was seeing something scary—a ghost, maybe, or a bunch of angry ostriches out of their pen. I shuddered a little and rolled my eyes like a horse does when it's been spooked by something.

That's when Mary Mason let out a little contemptuous snort of laughter. It was pretty quiet but it set Walter and the other kids to snickering. I could see them out of the corner of my eye, trying so hard not to laugh that their shoulders were beginning to shake.

I don't know what kind of disease I was supposed to be sick from, but laughter must be like measles, because it jumped from the other kids right over to me. I felt a laugh bubbling up and squeezed my lips together hard to keep it back. Nell, who had reached the part of the scene where Jack came in and she shoved a gold watch at him and begged him to go fetch the doctor, shot me a look but didn't interrupt her weeping and wailing. I frowned hard to push down the laugh but it was like a sneeze, determined to come out. It burst out of me like the bark of a coyote.

"CUT!" hollered Mr. Corrigan, tearing at his hair. "Pearl, you can't laugh. And stop rolling your eyes around. You look like a rabid dog."

Well, that did it. The other kids burst out with guffaws. Except Mary, who just smirked at me with her mean eyes.

We tried it again, but it was worse this time. I angled my gaze so I couldn't see Mary or the other kids, but I kept hearing smothered snorts from their side of the room. And Mr. Corrigan's words had stuck a picture in my head. I kept imagining myself foaming at the mouth like a mad dog. Another dratted laugh rushed up my throat and belched out into the room.

"CUT!"

Again. I felt chilled inside. I knew film cost a pretty penny and it was my fault we were wasting it. I didn't dare look at Gordy for fear I'd see disappointment in his eyes at my wastefulness.

"All right, this isn't working," said Mr. Corrigan, sounding exasperated. "I need a sick child who looks like a sick child, not a snakebit mare." He studied the kids ranged against the wall.

"You, with the curls," he said, pointing at Mary. "Can you play sick and not laugh?"

"Why, yes, sir," said Mary, looking up at him with big ostrichy eyes. "I'm sure I can."

"All right, then. Pearl, trade places with—what's your name?"

"Mary Mason, sir."

"Mary. Go ahead and climb in the bed. Pearl, you stand over there behind the boys. And not a peep from any of you, do you hear?"

So there I was, fired from my second motion picture role ever, my part ripped out from under me by that simpering Mary Mason.

The worst part was, she was *good.*

I'd die before I'd admit it out loud, but when she turned her face toward the camera it was pale and drawn like she was wasting away and might die any second. Her eyes were big as saucers and full of pain and sorrow. There weren't any sneaky laughs lurking inside me now. Mary looked so deathly ill I might have worried about her—if she'd been anyone but Mary Mason.

Besides, the second Mr. Corrigan called "Cut!"— happily this time, because he'd gotten what he wanted—Mary shot me a look of smug triumph.

If I *had* been a rabid dog, I'd have bitten her.

Chapter 20

I would have hung around the Flying Q crowd every day, if my folks had let me. But some days the company went far out into the wild country east of town and Mama wouldn't let me tag along. Frank said Mr. Corrigan had an eye for dramatic scenery. He would find a craggy hill with a lone tree, say, and make up a story to happen in front of it. Lots of times he shot the end of the story first and then went back and figured out the events leading up to it.

That seemed like a curious way to tell a story, if you asked me.

But I guess it worked all right, because Frank said word was Mr. Corrigan's bosses back east were pleased with the reels he'd been sending them. In nine weeks he had directed seven whole pictures—all but one of them featuring my brothers, as cowboys, horse thieves, kidnappers, train robbers; and two of them featuring me. (Counting the one where Mary Mason took over my sickbed part.)

Frank knew more than ever about the picture-making business because I'd kept my promise and asked Gordy if he could have a turn at the crank. Gordy went one better and taught him how to look through the eyehole and fiddle with the focusing mechanism. Frank was in hog heaven. He took to camera operating like a duck to water. Gordy, amiable as ever, answered all his questions and then some.

And some of Gordy's kind manners must have rubbed off on my brother, because Frank hardly ever condescended to me now when I asked him questions. He talked to me like I was his equal, even though he was five years older. I liked the Gordy version of Frank so much that I didn't even mind how much time they spent talking. If I was hanging around near the camera, Gordy included me in anything he had to say. Or rather, it was more like he included Frank in *our* conversations. I appreciated being treated like a *person* instead of a pesky kid—even if it was a little odd coming from Frank, who had always seemed so many miles above me. It was as if Jezebel had suddenly started treating me like another ostrich.

I was anxious for the finished pictures to come to town, and desperately hopeful I'd be taken to see them. It took time, Frank reminded me, for the studio to fix up the film so people could watch it. They had to add those cards with words on them to show what the actors were saying.

"What if you can't read?" I wanted to know.

Frank shrugged. "You figure it out, I guess."

"Do you think Mama and Papa will take me to see our pictures?" I asked him. This was the question that burned in my mind night and day.

"You sure you want them to?" Frank grinned. He meant because of my perilous horseback ride.

"Maybe not that one," I said.

But it was the one I wanted to see most of all.

Chapter 21

On days when Flying Q was filming in town, I raced through my chores and washed my face extra hard—anything to persuade Mama to let me go watch. I was amazed at Mr. Corrigan's inventiveness. You'd think he would have run out of stories after the first couple of weeks, but he kept coming up with new kinds of danger to put Nell or Jack in, and new dastardly deeds for Bart and my brothers to carry out.

One day the bad guys trapped Nell in a building and knocked over a lantern on the way out, starting a fire. At least, that's what Mr. Corrigan said would happen. He wasn't about to stick his star actress in a real fire on purpose. He paid a rancher to let him burn up an old, rotting shed while Gordy filmed it. I wasn't allowed to hang around that day, which rankled. I would have liked to see the flames roar up.

But I was there when they filmed the parts with Nell screaming out the second-story window of the Coopers' house. It was the same kind of old, weathered wood as the burned-up shed. Somehow, Mr. Corrigan's studio people would mix the two stretches of film together to make it look like the fire was happening in Nell's building.

Nell stuck her head out the open window and screamed bloody murder.

"Heeelp! Someone help me!" she wailed. It was a pity nobody would be able to hear her in the picture—her shrieks made my blood run cold. But there was one thing I couldn't understand.

"Why's she just standing there hollering like a goof?" I asked Gordy. "If it were me, I'd jump out the window."

"Jack's going to come along to save her."

"But how does she know that? It's silly to just stand around and hope somebody shows up to save you."

Mr. Corrigan turned and gave me a sharp look. I gulped. I hadn't realized I was talking loud enough for him to hear me.

"She's two stories up, kid. What's she supposed to do, jump down and break her neck?"

"Aw, it ain't that high. I've jumped out of our barn loft before and I bet it's at least as high as that old window," I boasted. "It's duck soup. Of course that's when the hay is piled high. Gotta have a good cushion or you'll crack your head open."

The way Mr. Corrigan was staring at me, I started to wonder if I was looking like a mad dog again. But then he said, "Gordy—cut. I have a thought," and went into the house to talk to Nell.

Watching them in the window was like watching a moving picture, I guessed—I could see the direction of their conversation but couldn't hear what they were saying. But it was easy to follow the thrust of the discussion. Mr. Corrigan leaned out and looked down, and he was pointing at the ground and gesturing to Nell. She peered down too and then reared up, shaking her head, looking at him like this time *he* was the rabid dog.

Her voice climbed to where I could hear it.

"Not if you paid me double!"

I saw Mr. Corrigan scrunch his mouth sideways. He was disappointed, I could tell.

"Aw, she's too scared to jump," I muttered. I was disappointed, too. I thought Nell had more gumption.

"Not too scared. Too smart," said Gordy companionably.

"Hmph." I could see his point.

"You sound unconvinced, lass." Gordy's eyes twinkled at me. I liked the way his smile squinched up higher on one side of his mouth than the other.

Mr. Corrigan came

back out of the house. His hair was spiked up like a yucca plant.

"Nothing doing," he said glumly. "I can't talk her into it."

And then he looked at me.

Chapter 22

I'd like to make out as if I was death-defyingly heroic, but the truth is, jumping out that window really was duck soup. Mr. Corrigan talked Mr. Cooper into letting him pile a heap of hay under the window, and then I stood in the window and screamed my head off just like Nell had done. Then Mr. Corrigan told me to look back over my shoulder like I was seeing the flames draw closer, and after that I just hopped right out and fell in the haystack. Easy as pie.

Mr. Corrigan said he'd have to go back to his hotel and think up a new story that put a little girl in the burning building instead of a beautiful young woman. I was afraid Nell would be sore at me for

taking over her part, but she laughed and said she admired my pluck.

"Don't worry about me, sugar," she told me. "Mr. C.'ll use me in the picture somehow. I sell tickets."

She was right. In the new version of the story, which we filmed during the next couple of days, I was her little sister and Nell came in from the fields just in time to see me jump out the window. She carried on a bit, fussing over me and hugging me tight, and then stood wringing her hands as she pretended to watch our house burn down. The rest of the story seemed a little silly to me. The older sister decided that since the two were now homeless, she had no choice but to marry a low-down dirty scoundrel who'd been pestering her for years. Just in the nick of time, a young man— Jack, of course—galloped up and stopped the wedding. It turned out he was her long-lost sweetheart, who had gone north to pan for gold, and now he was back with his saddlebags stuffed with sacks of money.

Since the only other thing besides jumping out the window the little sister had to do was look mournful during the almost-wedding and jubilant at the return of the sweetheart, I got through my scenes without a hitch. The jubilant part was especially easy: I just imagined what Mary Mason would say when she found out I'd landed another part.

Chapter 23

After that, Mr. Corrigan seemed to come up with all kinds of parts for me. I was a rich man's daughter taken captive by kidnappers; a miner's daughter trapped in a cave-in; a farmer's daughter galloping for help in the face of stock thieves. No more sickbed scenes, though. If he needed a tragically ill child, he sent for Mary Mason.

But audiences preferred adventure tales, he said. And adventuring, it turned out, was a Donnelly specialty. My brothers got bolder and bolder with the feats they were willing to undertake for a picture. Once, Mr. Corrigan hired an automobile and filmed Bill racing alongside it on horseback and then vaulting right into the auto. When they practiced it, Bill made it look so easy I was hankering to try it myself. But then when they did it for real, with the camera rolling, Bill shot off the horse a little too fast and came down more on top of the automobile than in it. Luckily, he got a good grip on the edge of the windshield or he might have rolled right off the hood and under the wheels. As it was, he smashed his face and bloodied his nose. Ike said it was a wonder he hadn't broken it. Mr. Corrigan didn't say anything at all for about ten minutes. He

went as pale as the moon in a daytime sky and sent everyone home for the day.

But I heard him murmur to Gordy, "Did you get it?"

"I got it, boss."

"Good lad."

It was strange to think about people watching me and my brothers in the pictures—people in faraway cities, people I would never know or see. I tried to imagine some kid in Chicago or Philadelphia watching me jump out of the Coopers' second-story window. Would they wonder who I was? Would they be admiring or envious?

The idea gave me a creepy feeling like a lizard running up my spine. I discussed the matter with the ostriches, because I knew they wouldn't laugh at me. They might try to nip off my nose, but they wouldn't laugh.

"Mary Mason says she's going to be famous," I said to Jezebel, watching her flap her wings to warn the other birds away from the feed trough until she'd gotten her fill. "She says people all over the world will know her name."

Jezebel turned her head and eyed me sideways. She looked skeptical.

"She's pretty swell at crying," I said, "but I don't

know why you'd get famous for that. Anybody with a baby can stay home and watch it blubber for free. Why pay a nickel to watch some kid bawl?"

Jezebel bobbed her head on her snaky neck. She agreed with me, I could tell.

"I don't think I want to be famous," I told her. "But I'd put up with it if they'd let me keep doing stunts in the pictures. I wish they needed someone to jump out another window. It was fun, landing in all that hay."

Jezebel gave her wings an irritated flap. Something about her hostile gaze under those long ostrich eyelashes reminded me of the way Mary had glared at me the day Mr. Corrigan put me in a picture. And suddenly I realized why she'd been so mad. She'd been jealous. Jealous that I was going to be in a moving picture and not her. All this time she'd probably been dreaming of being a famous actress. And there I was, barely even aware such things as actresses existed.

"I wonder if Mary's been to the opera house," I mused aloud. "I bet she's seen lots of pictures." I thought about asking her. But no, why give her another chance to snub me?

Instead, I climbed up on a fence rail and reenacted

the jumping-out-the-window scene from my third picture. I hollered like I was falling four stories instead of four feet, landing in the soft dirt with a satisfying thud.

Jezebel frowned at me. She didn't approve of such shenanigans. But she didn't approve of much of anything, so that was all right.

Chapter 24

One morning Mama sent me to the post office to mail a letter she'd written her aunt in Colorado. I saddled Dinah, who was in a lively mood. Perfect. The faster we got to town, the longer I could hang around on Straight Street to see if anything interesting was happening.

It was one of those fresh, clear mornings when the sky is smooth and blue as a ribbon. The air was still cool on my skin; the day's heat hadn't set in yet. I'd likely bake on the way home, but for now it felt delicious, putting me in a lively mood of my own. I could tell Dinah was charmed by the weather; she cantered with her head held high and proud. A hawk sailed in lazy circles above us. Small finches with berry-colored heads darted in and out of bushes along the road, fussing at each other or singing hymns; I'd no idea which. A stout bull snake coiled on a warm stone lifted its head to watch us go by.

As we neared the edge of Lemon Springs, the bird chatter and leaf rustle all around was drowned out by people noises: men shouting to each other in the lumberyard, wagons groaning and rattling on the dusty road, kids hollering whose turn it was to go next, mothers hollering at the kids to stop squabbling. They sounded like the finches, only sharper.

The post office was a two-story red-brick building sitting by itself on a Straight Street block. The building was owned by the Lemon Springs Lemon Co., a fact announced in big white letters two feet high painted on the bricks across the top of the front wall. On the north side of the building, more big white letters shouted about shoes and gear and EVERYTHING USED ON A RANCH. A man in dusty pants and a dusty cap leaned against the white-framed windows reading a newspaper under the wide front-porch roof, which bore a small sign that said POST OFFICE. It always seemed funny to me that the post office sign was so little and the LEMON CO. sign was so huge. It was like some enormous tree, a live oak maybe, with a little mushroom at its base—but you knew the mushroom was connected underground to ten thousand more mushrooms all across the country.

I was about to walk through the mushroom's door when a big advertisement on the back of the dusty man's newspaper caught my eye.

I stared openmouthed at the two small photographs printed above the names of the pictures. One was a picture of Ike on horseback, wearing his black mustache and aiming his gun at someone outside the frame.

The other photo was of me.

Chapter 25

There I was in the window of the farmhouse, one leg over the sill, about to jump. That was me. My face, my leg.

It was real. Right there in the newspaper! I was in a moving picture, and people were going to see it. Strangers. Family. Mary Mason.

"Can I help you, missy?" the dusty man asked, startling me. He was eyeing me over the top edge of his paper.

"No, sir!" I blurted, embarrassed to have been caught gawking at my own photograph. At the same time, I couldn't help but wonder if he'd seen the photo. Would he recognize me?

I didn't know if I wanted him to. I felt my cheeks

go hot. The post office door opened and a woman came out. I scooted in behind her as the door swung shut. My heart was pounding like I'd just raced an ostrich. (They're freakishly fast, those birds. Maybe that's why they don't bother to use their wings for flying, just for flapping in my face to scold me.)

I think I got Mama's letter posted all right, but I couldn't say for sure. My head was whirling with the staggering *real*ness of that advertisement. Why, Mr. Corrigan's company had paid money to have it printed in the paper!

What if people didn't like the pictures? What if they saw right through my pretending? When Nell performed, you forgot it was acting. It was like she was a brand-new person actually living this experience, not an actress who put on new parts as easily as new hats. And the scary, scowling villain Bart was a whole different person from the Bart with the sideways grin, palling around with my brothers after the camera stopped rolling. Bill and Ike were teaching him how to fall off a horse without killing himself. But the second Mr. Corrigan yelled "Action!" the amiable, joking-around Bart would vanish and the murderous scoundrel would appear.

I walked a whole block down Straight Street before I remembered I'd left my horse tied outside the post office. I turned back to fetch her and bumped smack into Mary Mason.

"Ow!" she yelled, and her mother, a fearsome tower with an imposing scowl, snapped at me to watch where I was going. She was a tall, rail-thin woman with a long neck, reminiscent of an ostrich. Same angry eyes, same jutting-out chin. She seemed as likely to dart forward and nip me as Jezebel.

"Beg pardon," I mumbled, wanting to scoot around them and get back to Dinah. But then I froze in shock.

Mary was smiling at me with a big toothy grin like she was my best friend in the world. I eyed her suspiciously. I'd seen in that sickbed scene what a convincing actress she could be when she wanted to, almost as good as Nell.

"Why, don't you trouble yourself the slightest little bit, Pearl!" she said, her voice syrupy sweet. "What a lovely surprise, bumping into you."

"It is?" I asked, skeptical.

Her eyes flickered and it was like a window shade going up; for a second I could see the real Mary inside. Then the shade went back down and the Mary made of syrup and smiles returned.

"Yes, indeed," she chirped. "I wonder if you've heard the exciting news! Mr. Corrigan has asked me to appear in another one of his pictures! I'm to play a minister's daughter who helps tend the sick."

"Oh," I said, not sure how to respond. I knew that smile had to be an act. Under all that syrup was a pancake made of spite.

I figured she just wanted to gloat over me. Well, I wasn't about to give her the satisfaction. Thanks to Nell's tips, I was learning a thing or two about acting myself. I put on a big toothy smile of my own and gushed, "Well, how about that? Isn't that just the most *tremendous* news!"

In that moment I realized everybody's an actor at some point or other—pretty much every day, come to think of it. When Bill almost got killed vaulting from horseback into that auto, he acted like it was no big deal at all, nothing worse than stubbing a toe. After Dinah ran away with me, I acted nonchalant about it even though it was pretty scary. When I tried my hand at baking cookies last year, Ike gobbled his down with what sure looked like genuine enthusiasm and said it was positively indescribable. Then I bit into one myself and discovered something had gone terribly, terribly wrong. I must have mixed up the salt with the sugar, and I definitely didn't get all the eggshells when I was picking them out of the mixing bowl. (Chicken eggs are the devil to crack. Ostrich eggshell shards are big enough you can't possibly miss them.)

That means Ike was only pretending his cookie tasted good, to spare my feelings. Was acting (in real life, not for a moving picture) a kind of lying? A *kind* kind of lying? I'd need to think about this.

Anyway, what Mary and I were doing didn't have anything to do with kindness. She was pretending to be sweet to me when really she just wanted to gloat. And I was pretending sweet right back, so as not to give her the satisfaction of making me feel bad. And that was another curious thing—if she wanted me to feel bad in the first place, why go about it in that sneaky fake-smile way? Why not just get there directly like she usually did, with one of her mean-eyed glares?

All these thoughts swirled in my head as I stood

there having that smile-off with Mary. Her mother was smiling too, sort of—at least, it looked like a proud-mama smile wanted to shine out because of Mary's part in the picture, but it was like a rodeo bull trying to break through the gate; it couldn't get past the pinched-up set of her lips. Mary's smile was growing frowny at the edges. I don't think she was swallowing my syrup any more than I was swallowing hers.

"Well," I said cheerfully, wanting to be back on my horse away from this awkward scene, "I'd best be getting home. Congratulations on your swell news, Mary!"

I scooted around them as quick as I could and was on Dinah's back and almost to the edge of town before I remembered I'd wanted to poke around on Straight Street, maybe wander the rows at the feed-store, where the air smelled of sawdust and canvas, and the big sacks of feed let out puffs of grain dust when you punched them.

Oh well, I might as well head home. Dinah had traded in her lively mood for a pokey one, so home would be a while off. I had plenty to keep my mind busy while I rode. When you're alone on the chaparral, just you and your horse, that's the best time for pondering. Dinah minded her own business and didn't give a fig about mine. Horses don't *act;* they just are. Cattle, too. Dogs, cats. Chickens. Ostriches— hmm. Most of the time an ostrich lets you know exactly what she thinks, with no regard at all for your feelings. But every now and then I've seen an ostrich pretend to be chummy just so you drop your guard and get close enough for a good nip.

Same kind of acting as Mary Mason's, come to think of it.

Chapter 26

What with the blizzard of thoughts about smiles and kind-acting and mean-acting and ostrich-acting (same thing, I guess), I forgot about the whole point of Mary pretending to be chummy with me until later, after I'd watered Dinah and stowed her saddle and left her in the north pasture with Apple. So Mary was going to be in another picture. *Why her and not me?* I wondered, heading for the washbasin in the lean-to outside the kitchen. A couple of pangs of hurt pricked at me—Had Mr. Corrigan decided I wasn't good enough? Was he tired of me?—but then I remembered Mary in that sickbed scene and I had to admit there were things she did better than I could.

I shook the water off my hands and went to look for a snack.

"What's ailing you, Pearl?" Grandma said, barring my path into the kitchen. "Indigestion? I can mix you up some bicarb and water."

"No, ma'am!" I said hastily, shuddering at the thought. "I'm fine. Just hungry."

I tried to tack a little plaintive note to the last word, hoping Grandma would offer a slice of cake or maybe some doughnuts. But Grandma saw right through me. She snorted and pointed to the basket of apples on the worktable.

Doesn't matter how fine an actress you are—you can't fool your grandmother.

I took my apple to the courtyard and sat in the cool shade, leaning my back against our well. A little black phoebe alit on the back of Grandma's patio rocking chair, where she liked to sit and do her sewing on summer evenings. It tilted its pointy head to eye me warily. It had no need to worry; I felt worn out with questions and wondering, too worn out to move.

I knew one thing for sure: Whatever this new picture was about, it wouldn't involve Mary risking her neck. Mary Mason wouldn't risk breaking a finger-nail, let alone her neck.

⌒

Turned out I needn't have worried. Mr. Corrigan wasn't finished with me. My brothers came home from another day of cowpunching for the camera with a message from Mr. C. New picture, Monday morning, standard rate, wear shoes.

Shoes! Sounded like a fancy part. All the ranchers' daughters and poor urchins I'd played so far ran around barefoot. (The best way to run around, in my opinion.)

Come Monday morning, Mary and I both got a big surprise: We were to play sisters!

Mary gave me a steely glare, her lips pinching tighter and tighter until she looked quite a lot like her mother, that day on the street. Her hair was curled into long sausages and her blue dress was crisp and fresh-pressed. I could feel her assessing my flyaround hair and my patched boy-pants. Well, let her stare. What did it matter what I was wearing? The costume lady would have something for me to change into. She had a whole trunkful of clothes back at the rooms the picture people used as their offices, at the Henderson Hotel in Lemon Springs.

"I don't think we look at all like sisters," said Mary primly.

I shrugged. "Ike and Bill don't look anything alike, and they're brothers."

"Hmm," said Mary. You could tell she was dying to add a *-ph* at the end. *Hmph*, like an irritated horse.

"All right, young ladies," said Mr. Corrigan, rushing up to us in his usual hurry. "Here's the scene. You're orphan sisters, alone in the world and utterly devoted to each other."

Mary and I cast each other a glance. I guessed we were going to find out if either one of us really could act as well as Nell and Bart.

"You're down to your last nickel, about to starve. Then you see a sign announcing an exhibition for a hot-air balloon. You reckon all sorts of fancy folks will turn up for it, and maybe you can talk one of them into giving you some work. We'll shoot that part today. The fella with the balloon should be here tomorrow."

"The balloon," I murmured, feeling dazed. Mr. Corrigan was bringing in a real hot-air balloonist? Was there any chance—my heart quickened—was there any chance he was planning to send us up in it?

He wasn't, though. Not *us*.

Just me.

Chapter 27

I didn't know I'd been holding my breath until I heard Mary let hers out. Her eyes were wide, and for a second I thought she was furious that she wasn't going up in the balloon, too. But then I saw the panic in them, like a horse rearing away from a rattlesnake. She'd been terrified. Her whooshing breath was a gust of relief.

Mr. Corrigan was eyeing me. "You all right with this, Pearl? I have something pretty nervy in mind for you, but if anyone can do it, you can."

I swallowed hard. What could be nervier than going up in a hot-air balloon?

Coming down from one, it turned out. The story

Mr. Corrigan had dreamed up had the sisters wandering around at the balloon exhibition, asking for work and being refused over and over. They wander over to gawk at the balloon with a bunch of other kids. The balloon man is having his picture taken in front of it, preening before the admiring crowd. A rotten little boy in the crowd—to be played by Walter—snatches a rag doll out of the younger sister's hands. Mary, of course. The doll was made by their mother; it's all they have left of her. As a joke, the stinker of a boy tosses the doll into the balloon basket. The older, bolder sister—me, naturally—scrambles into the basket to retrieve it. The balloonist notices and starts hollering for the girl to get out. A scuffle breaks out—grown-ups and kids shouting and shoving—and in the ruckus someone knocks loose the tether rope and the balloon sails up into the sky with the older sister in it.

"Now, Pearl," said Mr. Corrigan. "We won't really send you up alone. Your mother would flay me alive." His mouth screwed up sideways under his mustache. "She might anyway, when she sees the picture. But I'll cross that bridge when I come to it."

His plan was to have the real balloon operator crouch down in the basket before they released the rope. It would shoot up into the sky, but not too far—he wanted the camera to get a good, long look at my terrified face.

Terror wouldn't take much acting, under those circumstances. But it was exciting, too—a ride in a real hot-air balloon.

"Now, what would be *really* swell," Mr. Corrigan mused, gazing at some invisible movie playing in his head, "would be to have you toss the anchor rope over the side of the basket and shinny down it. But—" He sighed regretfully. "But I suppose that would be too much to ask of anyone, even a spunky gal like you."

To this day I don't know if he was being sincere, or if maybe Mr. Corrigan was the best actor of us all.

Chapter 28

It's fitting that Mr. Corrigan was always calling out
"Action!" to signal to Gordy and the actors that it
was time to start filming a scene. *Action* could have
been his middle name. He barreled directly from
telling us the balloon story to setting us up to shoot
the first scene. There wasn't time to wonder or
worry about the balloon ride; I had to learn my part
in the first bit of the story. Which meant working
with Mary Mason—which was maybe more nerve-
wracking than the idea of climbing out of a hot-air
balloon.

The costume lady got us changed, and fussed
with our hair. At least, she fussed with mine. Mary's
perfect ringlets defied any interloping. Personally, I

didn't see how it made sense for a poor orphan kid to have fancy curls and a hair ribbon, but I kept my opinion to myself. I reckoned I might tell Jezebel about it when I got home, just to see the disdain in her eyes. Ostriches make a satisfying audience if you pick the right story.

We practiced the scene a couple of times—huddling together on the ground against a barn wall, the Mary-sister crying and the me-sister comforting her. Both of us staring into the camera with big woebegone eyes. I pulled a little money purse out of my pocket and opened it, acting sorrowful and worried because it was empty. Turned it upside down and shook it, as if that could conjure up one last coin to buy us some bread.

"Oh, sister, what will become of us!" Mary said, her eyes welling up with tears. I had to admit—way down in a secret part of myself—it was pretty impressive, the way she could cry on cue. We practiced three times and she welled up like clockwork on every one. By the time we were ready to film the scene, Mary almost had me believing we *were* two poor little orphan sisters.

It was the strangest thing. Before Flying Q sailed into town, I hadn't given Mary much thought. Before this summer I couldn't have said whether I liked her or not; I barely knew her.

But then Mr. Corrigan happened, and Mary spent the whole summer glaring daggers at me. You don't exactly develop affectionate feelings about a person who looks at you like she wishes a piano would fall on your head.

The more she didn't like me, the more I didn't like her. That's basic arithmetic.

So I expected that performing in a picture with her would be worse than having her watch me—that those daggers would shoot right out of her eyes and make me flub my part.

But instead, there she was crying real tears, looking so scared and pitiful I couldn't help but put my arm around her shoulders and assure her everything would be okay. The scareder and sadder she was, the fiercer I felt. She wasn't an ostrich at all. She was a lamb, and it was up to me to look after her.

For just a moment I forgot all about the camera and Gordy and the other crew members and gawkers watching. I forgot to wonder whether Mr. Corrigan was yanking his hair clean out (sign of a bad scene) or smoothing his mustache, his eyes gleaming (sign of a good one). I even forgot myself. I wasn't Pearl, tender of ostriches and sneaker of manzanita jam. I was a brave orphan child with a little sister to look after.

I shook out the empty purse, hoping against hope. No miracle coins tumbled out from the lining. I glanced at my sister and saw the tears spill down her cheeks. I felt my lips bunch sideways the way they do when you're thinking hard. I *was* thinking hard. There had to be a way out of this fix. I jumped to my feet and paced around a little, and then the poster tacked to the side of the barn caught my eye: HOT-AIR BALLOON DEMONSTRATION, to be held in the town square—why, this very day!

My sister's eyes filled with hope as I laid out my plan. I didn't use many words (somewhere way underneath the orphan girl was Pearl, who knew nobody watching would hear what she said), but I pointed to the poster and gestured to Mary, and she clasped her hands and looked hopeful. In fact, she radiated hope and trust in me, and I knew she was counting on me to find us work at the balloon exhibition. She clutched my hands and I squeezed a message of confidence into hers. We'd been through so much together, and we'd get through this, too—hunger and poverty and worry. She was my sister, and together we would find a way to save ourselves.

When Mr. Corrigan called "Cut!" I just about jumped out of my skin. I'd forgotten we were filming. My sweet little sister flashed back into prickly Mary Mason. We were still clutching each other's hands, and now we dropped them, a little embarrassed. But something was different. The tears were gone from Mary's eyes—but so were the daggers. In their place was—I hardly know how to describe it—a kind of crackling electricity, like lightning. I couldn't explain it, but I recognized it. I felt it, too.

Like lightning, it was gone two seconds later. Mary's cool, appraising look was back and I felt flustered and foolish. She was still Mary Mason, armed with an endless supply of eye daggers. She sauntered off to get a drink of water, looking pleased as punch with herself. She'd given a great performance, and she knew it.

Fine. We weren't any likelier to suddenly become fast friends than a golden doubloon was likely to fall out of the empty prop coin-purse.

But something had changed. I didn't like Mary Mason, but I . . . respected her. And I had liked acting with her. Loved it, in fact. The little flashes of this-feels-real that I'd experienced once or twice filming other scenes—this time had been more than a flash. For a few minutes, I really was that girl. She had a whole different life from me, a different history. For a few minutes, I walked in someone else's skin, and it was magical.

Chapter 29

At home that evening I was feeding the ostriches when an odd shadow rolled across the yard: a shape too perfectly round to be a cloud. I looked up and felt my stomach jump. It was a hot-air balloon! *My* hot-air balloon! I felt almost dizzy. It was really happening. Mr. Corrigan had made it happen.

The balloon gleamed in stripes of red and orange against the deepening blue sky. A basket dangled beneath it, looking about the size of a basket you'd grab to go berry picking. But then I spotted a man looking out over the side and realized how big the basket must be, really.

To my astonishment the man saw me watching

and waved. The balloon was sailing toward Lemon Springs. It hadn't occurred to me the balloonist would *fly* in, but of course it made sense. What was he supposed to do, put the balloon on a train?

I hastily dumped the rest of the ostrich feed in a heap on the ground, too excited to spread it in the trough. Then I lit out for the house before Jezebel had time to scold me.

Mama and Grandma were already outside staring up at the balloon. Mama's hands were covered in flour and Grandma had an apron full of chicken feed. The hens clucked around her feet, tilting their befuddled heads, but Grandma was too enchanted by the sight of the balloon to notice. I couldn't help but laugh—seemed I wasn't the only one skimping on chores this morning.

"What on earth is a thing like that doing here?" Mama wondered.

"What in the sky, you mean," said Grandma dryly.

"It's Mr. Corrigan," I blurted. Two pairs of eyes looked at me in confusion. "I mean, not in the balloon. He hired it. For a picture."

I hadn't had the guts to tell them yet. And now

it seemed like the information was on the tardy side, with the balloon sailing through the sky halfway to heaven. I felt a wave of nervousness. I hadn't been any too sure in the first place whether my parents would let me film the balloon scene Mr. C. had in mind. Now, seeing how impossibly high it was, I felt all too sure I knew what they'd say.

I gulped. "I was going to tell you at supper," I said. "I mean, ask you. See, Mr. Corrigan wrote a story—it's a corker, honest!—about . . ."

Both Mama's and Grandma's eyebrows were raising, slowly, in perfectly matched expressions.

"About?" asked Mama.

"Well, about a girl who goes up in a—"

"I told you that man was out of his mind," snapped Grandma, glaring at Mama. Mama was crackling the same look at me.

"A girl," she said. "And I suppose we can guess just exactly which girl he has in mind."

"It'll be quite safe, Mama!" I assured her. "He promised. The balloon won't go up as high as that. . . ." I looked up to point, but the red-and-orange globe had drifted to the west, headed toward town. It must have been close, because it seemed to be sitting lower in the sky than a minute before. I was itching to jump on my horse and go see it. All the town kids—and grown-ups, too, most likely—would be clustering around to watch it set itself down in the square. How maddening that I would be one of the last people in town to see it up close!

But I roped my wits back in and turned to the daunting task of persuading my family to let me shoot this picture.

"Mr. Corrigan said it'll just go up a little way, not real high," I explained. "And the balloon man will be there, running everything. All I have to do is look over the side of the basket. And then . . ." I swallowed, but I knew I might as well get it all out in the open right away. "And then I'll climb down a rope to the ground, easy as pie."

"YOU'LL WHAT?" screeched my mother and grandmother in unison.

"It'll be just like swinging on a rope from the barn loft," I gabbled. I'd been thinking about it all afternoon and had hit upon this as my best chance of getting a *yes*. "Or at the swimming hole!"

"Mm-hmm," said my mother crisply. "Same way a rattlesnake bite is 'just like' a nip from a garter snake."

My heart sank. This wasn't going well.

And then, to my surprise, my grandmother came to my rescue.

"How high is 'not real high'?" she asked.

"Mother!" gasped Mama. "You can't be serious—"

"I'm just asking questions, Anna," Grandma said, her tone a trifle reproving. I had to squeeze back a smile; it was always funny when Grandma got stern with Mama like she was still her little girl.

Mama blinked at her and then her eyes narrowed.

She began brushing the flour off her hands. "Tell you what. Mother, if you'll finish my biscuits, I'll take Dinah and go have a chat with Mr. Corrigan. I'd like to hear about this ridiculous scheme from the horse's mouth."

Chapter 30

It about killed me that Mama didn't take me with her. She told me to help Grandma with supper, since she had to interrupt her work for this non-sense. I wanted to plead to go along, but I knew I'd better be as cooperative as possible. I mustered my syrupiest Mary Mason voice and said, "Yes, ma'am. Happy to."

Mama's eyebrows quirked at me suspiciously but she didn't say anything. And I barely made a peep myself all the rest of the day. It's hard to talk when your heart is in your throat.

After several eternities she came home—laughing.

"That man," she said. "I believe he could sell water to a pond."

Somehow, miraculously, he had talked her into saying *yes*. He'd also convinced her to consider having a telephone put in. This was a staggering development.

"Mr. Corrigan made a fair point. If Pearl is going to keep making pictures, I need a faster way to give him a piece of my mind. I can't be traipsing into town all the time."

She delivered this news over supper, and the ensuing hullabaloo over the telephone, which Frank and Ike had been clamoring after for months, crowded out any further discussion of my balloon stunt. That suited me fine. I didn't want anyone rustling up new doubts and worries. Truth was, I had more than a few of my own.

Ike and Frank fixed me a practice rope tied from the branch of a tree, a good way up. We took turns climbing up and shinnying down. Bill stood below, ready to catch me if I slipped. The rope swayed in a rather unnerving way as you inched downward, as if it were a live thing—a snake, maybe. But I wasn't about to let my brothers outdo me. I could hang on and scooch down just as well as they could. The trick, I discovered, was not letting yourself slide, not if you wanted to keep the skin on your hands.

When it came time to go to town the next morning, Mama and Grandma joined me and my brothers
at the stable.

"You're coming!"

"Of course we are," said Grandma, reaching into her skirt pocket and taking out a set of rosary beads— her best one, made of shiny black onyx. "Someone's got to be there to pray for you if you fall and break your head."

"Mother!" gasped Mama.

"Oh hush," chuckled Grandma. "I'm only teasing. Pearl's like a cat. Lands on her feet."

"Where's Papa?" I asked.

Mama made a wry face. "Not coming. Too scared, the poor man."

"Papa, *scared?*" I was incredulous.

"Just don't fall, Pearl," said Mama softly. "Your father would never forgive himself."

The balloon field was abuzz with people, with the big striped globe in the center like a hive. Seemed like half the town was hanging around to gawk at the spectacle, conveniently saving Mr. Corrigan the trouble of rustling up people to play visitors at the balloon exhibition in the picture. He wanted to get the up-in-the-air part filmed first thing, in case the weather turned. (This brought some knowing smiles from Lemon Springs natives. Summer weather seldom turns anything but *more hot*. But you couldn't expect a Chicago man to know that.)

So we skipped over the part of the story where the sisters mill around asking townspeople for work. Since the film was going to be cut up anyway to splice the title cards in, we'd have no problem coming back to that later. Mr. Corrigan had us set up for the bit where the mean boy tosses the Mary-sister's doll into the balloon. It took a lot more practice—and a lot more hollering from Mr. Corrigan—than usual before we were ready to do it on camera. I began to worry he was going to yank himself bald. I'd never been in a scene with such a crowd before, and most of them were first-timers who didn't know how to behave. It was the strangest thing to realize I knew more about making moving pictures than most of the grown-ups in Lemon Springs!

"Action!"

Snatch—Walter grabbed Mary's doll and tossed it into the balloon basket. Just as we'd practiced, I scrambled in after the doll. The balloonist (Bart in a top hat, not the real balloon man) shouted at me and pushed his way through the mob of kids to order me out of the basket. Walter stumbled backward against the balloon's tether rope.

That was all for that scene. Mr. Corrigan ordered all the Lemon Springs folks except my family out of the field for the next shot. It was time for me to fly.

Chapter 31

The balloon man (the real one) was, as promised, crouching out of camera view in the bottom of the basket. He'd introduced himself, Mr. Jedediah P. Irving, to me with great solemnity before we started rehearsing the crowd scene. When I clambered into the basket, he had to scooch back hastily so I didn't land on top of his head. I wanted to apologize but that would be out of character for the role I was playing. I wasn't Pearl; I was an orphan girl climbing into an empty basket.

Mr. Irving had rigged his controls so he could adjust the flame that made the balloon fly without standing up in his usual position. He'd also shown me how to avoid getting scorched. As long as I stayed at the rim of the basket, I'd be in no danger, he assured me.

Of course, the trouble was I wouldn't be staying at the rim of the basket. I'd be climbing over it to scoot down the rope.

But before I could come down, we had to go up. And after some instructions from Mr. Corrigan and a good-luck wave from Gordy, it was time. I waved at Mama and Papa. *Wait! Papa?* He'd come after all. He was scrunching his hat between his hands so fiercely I worried it would never get its shape back. He looked so worried I wanted to jump out of the basket and throw my arms around him.

But it was too late for jumping out, and there was no more time to think about my folks. At Mr. Irving's command, helpers loosed the tether ropes (for real, this time). Mr. Irving fiddled with a valve and the basket gave a sudden lurch. My stomach, deciding at the last second that it would prefer to stay as close to the ground as possible, plummeted to my toes. The trees and buildings across the square began to sink. No, of course that wasn't it; they were safe on the ground like always. We were the ones rising into the air. Me, Mr. Irving, and the sunset-colored balloon.

Now that we were rising, I knew exactly what I was supposed to do. Mr. Corrigan had run me through my movements before we left the ground. It wasn't practical to send the balloon up and down for rehearsals, so this take was the real thing. I had to get it right.

I clutched the edge of the basket where Mr. Corrigan had marked it. My job was to crane my head over and look down. Gordy had the camera set where it would catch my face as we went into the air, as long as I leaned out far enough.

Mary's doll was still in my hand, and when I looked down to see the ground zooming away from us, I almost dropped the doll right on the camera. The town square was turning into a patchwork quilt below me, and Mama and Papa and Grandma were dolls on the quilt. I could see all of Straight Street sprawling beneath us, and my school, and our church, and in the distance, good old Mount Caracol, solidly hunkered to the ground.

We sailed pretty high. The plan was to get a shot of the balloon way up, and then we'd drop lower to where I could scramble down the rope without breaking my neck if I fell. Just a leg or two, probably.

It was pretty hard to be the orphan girl in that

basket. I half wished Mary were here with me—it was so much easier to make the scene feel real when she was in it. But nope, this one was up to me.

I don't know exactly how high we went. Two or three miles, it felt like. The air was bracingly cool up here. A crow flew past—beneath us. The world was spread out below in soft ripples, with here and there the dark scratch of a canyon. I could see all the way to the sea, a dark-blue stripe on the patchwork quilt, spangled with flecks of light.

And then, just when I was forgetting to be scared—dazzled by the beautiful world below us—Mr. Irving twitched his controls and we began to sink. Slowly, gently, like an ostrich feather drifting to the ground.

Oh, but not all the way down. The ground was still far below us when Mr. Irving did some more lever-twitching and said, "All right, kid. I can hold her steady for a few minutes. Sure you want to get down by the rope? Seems mighty chancy to me."

"It'll be duck soup," I said breezily, acting my face off.

Now I had to put Orphan Girl back on. Mr. Corrigan had told me just what he wanted:

Lean over the side and look terrified. Easy.

Wave my arms around and look up, then down, and shriek a little, like you'd expect a kid to do if she found herself going up in a balloon by accident. Easy.

Wring my hands; reach out plaintively for Mary. Easy.

(Later, Mr. Corrigan would film Mary plaintively reaching up toward the sky for me.)

Now I was supposed to discover the anchor rope coiled in the basket and get a bold, scrappy look on my face. Easy.

Fling the rope over the side of the basket and watch it fall. Easy.

Climb over the side and shinny down the rope.

Not so easy.

Not duck soup. More like ostrich soup.

"Now just shinny down the rope!" Mr. Corrigan's voice boomed up through the megaphone.

I looked down the dangling rope. I tried to tell myself it wasn't all that far, not really. Not so different from my practice sessions with my brothers in the tree at home, but this time there was no Bill waiting to catch me if I fell.

I grabbed tight to the rope and put a knee over the lip of the basket. This orphan girl had better get back to her sister.

I wrapped my legs tight around the rope and, heart pounding, lowered myself inch by inch, hand under hand. Sometimes my hands slid a little and I felt the rope burning into them. But I squeezed as hard as I could, ignoring the sting in my palms. Better to lose a little skin than a whole life. I found I had to angle my head just so or else the rope rubbed against my cheek. I was figuring out a lot of things in a hurry up here in the wild air.

When I got to the bottom of the rope, I was still dangling six or seven feet above the ground. Mr. Corrigan was shouting instructions to me through his big megaphone. I could hear him a lot better now, but I wasn't sure that was a good thing. He was telling me to let go of the rope and jump the rest of the way. While looking like a fearless and determined orphan girl, of course. I think I got the determined part pretty well, but I don't know about fearless. I hoped the camera wouldn't capture the terror I'd been feeling since I climbed over the side of the basket.

My feet hit the ground and the air whooshed out of my lungs. My heart was hammering so loudly I could hardly hear a thing at first—and then I caught

the cries swelling up from the crew and all the on-lookers. The townspeople crowding the street be-yond the square cheered. Gordy cheered so hard he almost knocked over his camera. Of course, my brothers whooped loudest of all.

Papa didn't cheer. He just scooped me into his arms and squeezed tight.

When he finally let me go, I took a step and al-most keeled over—my legs were noodles. But I fig-ured that was a good sign. Better noodly legs than broken ones.

"What'd I tell you?" Mr. Corrigan demanded, sweeping his arms wide. "She's the nerviest girl in the world, our Pearl."

I caught sight of Mary in the throng. She was star-ing at me, but this time I couldn't find a single dagger in her eyes—just a smile.

Chapter 32

All this time, all these pictures, and I'd still never seen a single reel. Before Flying Q came to town, there wasn't any way to watch a moving picture in Lemon Springs. You had to go all the way to San Diego. After Mr. Corrigan and company had started filming in our neck of the woods, a mania for going to the pictures had swept across town, and now there were a few small makeshift nickelodeons—places where you could pay a nickel to watch a picture—in storefronts around Straight Street and Avocado Avenue. But I'd been so busy acting in pictures that I hadn't managed to talk anybody into taking me to see one! It was comical, really.

After the balloon stunt, the movie mania seemed

to infect Mama and Papa, too. They decided we'd all go together just as soon as Papa could spare time away from the cattle yard.

When the day came at last, Mama surprised me. She told me to put my shoes on, which had to mean either going to Mass or going to the city. And I knew we weren't going to Mass—not on a Tuesday afternoon.

We were taking the train into the city. Papa had decided that a rickety chair in a Lemon Springs storefront wouldn't do for such a momentous event. We were going to a real nickelodeon theater in San Diego. All of us, this time—Mama, Papa, Grandma, my brothers—and at long last, me.

Do you know, I don't remember one thing about the train ride? We might have been riding in the belly of a whale, for all I recall. It's too bad; this was the first time in memory that my whole family had taken the train together. It might not have been a grand cross-country trip to Baltimore like Juniper Howard's, but it was a pretty notable occasion.

I do remember the moment of walking up to the glassed-in booth outside a building, and a man in a red cap taking money from Papa and handing him tickets. We went through a big carved door, passing from blinding sunshine and street noise into a dim, cool, spacious place with rows and rows of plush seats, each one soft as a feather tick. A boy in a blue uniform led us to a row of empty seats, and we all filed in.

"Sit here, Pearl," said Ike, guiding me to a chair between him and Frank. Frank clattered his boots on the floor in excitement. Bill handed me a big greasy paper sleeve of peanuts. A huge white screen, maybe a sheet, took up the whole wall in front of us. Below the screen was a piano. A man in a yellow suit sat on its bench, drinking a bottle of sarsaparilla through a straw.

I tried to remember every detail of that theater— maybe that's why I lost the train ride; it was crowded out by the rustle of skirts and suits all around me here, the shuffle of dozens of pairs of shoes on the floor (carpeted in the aisles, hardwood under the seats), and a soft endless murmur of voices and throat-clearings and coughs, and a louder layer of kids fidgeting and giggling and drumming on seat backs.

Ike leaned over and squeezed my hand, which had a peanut in it, but neither of us cared about that at such a stupendous moment.

"Whaddaya think, Pearl? Grand enough for you?"

"The grandest!"

And then, suddenly, as if someone had given a signal: a hush. I saw that there *had* been a signal: the man at the piano had put his sarsaparilla bottle on the floor and turned to face the screen, his hands poised over the keys. Black dots appeared on the screen. The piano man began to play a jolly, lolloping tune. The screen went black, with white writing all over it—writing that flickered like the world going by outside a train window. THE PERILS OF PEARL, it read. A FLYING Q FILM COMPANY MOTION PICTURE.

My heart flickered, too.

Author's Note

The fictional town of Lemon Springs is loosely based on La Mesa, California, a small suburb east of San Diego, where I lived for eleven years. While there, I learned something that surprised me: for a short while in the early days of silent film, La Mesa was the home of a thriving movie studio. Today, we tend to think of Hollywood as the heart of American cinema. But for a brief period of time, it was La Mesa, when American Film Manufacturing Company sent a crew west to California. Known as Flying A Studios because of their winged logo, they pumped out more than 150 short films in just over a year.

The idea that an important chapter of cinema history unfolded literally in my backyard piqued my interest, and I began reading everything I could find about Flying A's time in La Mesa. When I discovered that many of the cowboys in Flying A's Westerns were real cowboys—ranchers and rodeo stars from San Diego County—I was hooked. Moviemaking was a brand-new endeavor, and our modern concept of professional stunt people was decades in the future. Director Allan Dwan recruited local cowboys because he needed fellas who could ride hard and fall soft. He also used professional actors—folks with theater and vaudeville backgrounds—for main roles. When I read about a group of rancher brothers who played bit parts in a number of Flying A films, a story began to take shape. But it was Pearl White, a silent-film star best known for *The Perils of Pauline*, who inspired me to learn more about the way movies were made in the earliest days of silent film.

At the turn of the twentieth century, film cameras and projectors were a breathtaking new technology. These days, when we can easily shoot video on our smartphones and tablet computers and share those moving images over the internet, it's hard to imagine a time when *moving* pictures were a shocking new concept, dazzling audiences around the world. The Frenchman Louis Le Prince is credited with inventing the first motion picture camera in the 1880s, but a number of inventors around the world had helped pave the way with various technological breakthroughs.

A few years (and many other inventions) later,

W. K.-L. Dickson, an employee of the famous American inventor Thomas Alva Edison, patented a machine called the Kinetoscope—a word that means "motion viewing." At the Chicago World's Fair in 1893, Edison introduced this technology to the American public, causing a huge stir. Kinetoscopes were large boxes with a peephole in the top. One person at a time could peer into the peephole and watch a short silent film. These first snippets of film didn't entertain the public with stories: the attraction was the technology itself. Crowds flocked to Kinetoscope parlors to peep through the hole and watch things like a man sneezing or a pair of boxers slugging it out in the ring.

By 1896, Edison and other inventors realized they could make a lot more money showing films to big crowds all at once instead of one at a time. This took some more technological innovation, but before long, audiences could watch short moving pictures in stage theaters and music halls. In some places, temporary movie theaters were set up in storefronts or even tents. Soon new theaters were being built especially for moving pictures. One of the first of these theaters was the Nickelodeon, which opened in Pittsburgh in 1905. Its name came from the price of a ticket—a nickel!

In no time at all, nickelodeons were popping up all over the United States. The public's enormous appetite for moving pictures sparked the development of dozens of film studios. Imaginative filmmakers began telling stories on film. Since there wasn't yet any technology that could add sound to moving pictures, these stories played out silently, with text cards interspersed in the action to show the audience what the characters were saying. Actors had to show emotions in a big, broad way, with vivid facial expressions and gestures.

Audiences especially loved adventure stories full of danger and suspense. Often, a story would be told in short weekly installments, much like network TV shows before the days of Netflix and binge-watching. These were called cinemas, and *The Perils of Pauline*, starring Pearl White, was one of the most popular, with twenty episodes. Each week, audiences flocked to the theater to see what kind of danger Pauline would find herself in this time around. The character of Pauline is a wealthy young woman whose guardian appoints his secretary, Koerner, to oversee Pauline's inheritance until she marries. But Pauline isn't ready to marry yet, and Koerner sees an opportunity to snatch her inheritance away—by getting rid of Pauline. Week after week, he devises a new way to off Pauline, and week after week, she manages to escape death in white-knuckle fashion. In the first installment of the film, Pauline winds up floating away in a hot-air balloon all by herself, with no way to land. Ever resourceful, she tosses the anchor rope over the side of the balloon's basket and climbs down the rope in her ankle-length dress. To my astonishment, I learned that Pearl White actually did this life-threatening stunt herself! In that moment, a heroine of my own began to take shape in my mind.

My Pearl is named in Pearl White's honor, but the balloon stunt is their only real overlap. Pearl White was younger than my Pearl when she got into the acting business, landing her first stage role at age six. Around age eighteen, she dropped out of high school to tour the Midwest with a theater company and went on to become a silent film star. Her adventure serials were wildly popular. And in those early days, Pearl White, like most other actors, was the one actually risking life and limb to perform jaw-dropping stunts—including racing cars and flying airplanes. Years later, the studio decided she was too valuable to risk and, from then on, a man in a wig did Pearl's stunts.

Another real-life figure who inspired a major character in my book is Allan Dwan. Mr. Corrigan is loosely based on Mr. Dwan, and he was great fun to write. Allan Dwan didn't set out to be a movie director—he studied engineering and worked for a lighting company before becoming a scriptwriter for a film studio.

The moviemaking business was in its infancy, and most early directors fell into the job rather than training for it. That was certainly the case with Allan Dwan. East

Coast and Midwestern film studios had begun sending crews to California, where the balmy weather made it easy to film outdoors year-round. California was also far away from Thomas Edison's infamous "patent thugs."

Allan Dwan was happily writing scripts in Chicago when a Flying A film crew went radio silent for weeks. Dwan's bosses sent him to California to track them down. What Allan found was a cast and crew sitting around in San Juan Capistrano twiddling their thumbs because the director had taken off for a spree in Los Angeles. Allan telegraphed the home office to say they'd better shut down the production and bring everyone home because they had no director.

The reply came back: YOU DIRECT.

Allan followed orders and began directing films. He moved operations to La Mesa Springs (later shortened to La Mesa) and explored the county for interesting scenery to use in the background of his films.

The La Mesa studio only lasted about a year. Eventually, Dwan felt he'd used up all the best locations and moved the studio up the coast to Santa Barbara, California. Flying A Studios filmed many, many more moving pictures there. In addition to filming around town, at the shore, and in the countryside, the company developed a studio where they could build their own sets.

This studio, the first of its kind, was located on a

former ostrich ranch. Ostrich farming was a fruitful endeavor in the early 1900s! Besides being sources of feathers, eggs, and meat, ostriches provided light entertainment for locals, who enjoyed watching them swallow oranges whole. In some places, you could even ride in a wagon pulled by an ostrich!

Naturally this intrigued me, and I decided Pearl's family needed to be in the ostrich-ranching business, as well as raising cattle and sheep. Ornery characters are fun to write, and ostriches are as ornery as they come.

The Donnelly family's bell timber was inspired by a real bell and shipwreck timber at the Hubert H. Bancroft Ranch House, a historical site in Spring Valley, California, just down the road from La Mesa. My kids and I used to drive past the Bancroft House every time we went to the doctor's office, so it was lots of fun to get to include it in a book. The bell post really was a timber salvaged from a shipwreck in 1856. Today, the house is a California Historical Landmark and appears on the National Register of Historic Places.

Allan Dwan went on to direct scores of films over the next several decades, transitioning from silent film to "talkies" when sound production came along. Some of his best-known works are *Sands of Iwo Jima* and *Heidi*, which starred Shirley Temple.

While inspired by real-life incidents like the *Perils of Pauline* balloon stunt, my account of Pearl Donnelly's adventures with Flying Q Studios is entirely fictional. Mr. Corrigan films in town a lot more often than Allan Dwan did. La Mesa doesn't have a Straight Street, but it does have a small mountain called Mount Helix, named after the spiraling shell of a snail, which inspired the name of my Mount Caracol.

A quote in Mollie Gregory's fascinating book *Stuntwomen: The Untold Hollywood Story* provided the title of my novel. In her passage on silent-film star Ruth Roland, Gregory mentions that Ruth was "dubbed 'one of the nerviest girls in pictures'" due to her willingness to perform dangerous stunts. The moment I read that quote, I knew I wanted to write about the nerviest girl in the world!

Acknowledgments

I'm indebted to Peter Bogdanovich's biography *Allan Dwan: The Last Pioneer* for its comprehensive study of this groundbreaking filmmaker.

Jim Newland of the La Mesa Historical Society was a tremendous help in pointing me toward resources about the history of La Mesa Springs and Flying A Studios. He even made it possible for me to watch one of Allan Dwan's one-reelers—filmed right there in the San Diego County chaparral that I love.

I would also like to thank my La Mesa friends Deirdre and Matthew Lickona, who gave me their guest room for a much-needed research trip after I moved to Oregon. Thanks, too, to Ron, Larry, Finch, Timmy, and Mo, who, at various points in time, listened to me chatter about sundry delightful tidbits I'd stumbled across in my research.

My family was beset with our own reel of adventures during the writing of this book, and I have deep appreciation for the small army of friends who helped us with our somewhat sudden interstate move. When I say we couldn't have done it without you, I'm being quite literal.

I'm immensely grateful for the friendship and encouragement I found in Michael Nobbs's Creative Circle. To all my morning planning-session pals: you're the artistic support community of my dreams, and I love you to pieces, even if you're bad for my art-supply budget.

To Helen McLaughlin—you were exactly what I needed. Thanks forever.

Special thanks to my wonderful agent, Liza Voges, and to my editor, Michelle Frey, whose keen insight, sound judgment, and unbridled enthusiasm are the biggest gifts a novelist could ask for.

Every book I write has my family threaded through and through. When I'm in my studio working, I'm listening to your laughter and banter on the other side of the door. Scott, my love—I hope you know how impossible all of this would be without you. Kate, Erin, Eileen, Steven, Kelly, and Sean: one million kisses, but nope, we can't get an ostrich.

Bibliography

Every carefully researched work of historical fiction draws from dozens of sources. The following books and resources were especially informative:

Abel, Richard. *Americanizing the Movies and "Movie-Mad" Audiences, 1910–1914.* Oakland: University of California Press, 2006.

Balshofer, Fred J., and Arthur C. Miller. *One Reel a Week.* Oakland: University of California Press, 1967.

Bogdanovich, Peter. *Allan Dwan: The Last Pioneer.* London: Studio Vista, 1971.

Bogdanovich, Peter. *Who the Devil Made It: Conversations with Legendary Film Directors.* New York: Ballantine Books, 1997.

Gregory, Mollie. *Stuntwomen: The Untold Hollywood Story.* Lexington: University Press of Kentucky, 2015.

"Hollywood: A Celebration of the American Silent Film. Episode 10: The Man with the Megaphone." Thames Television, 1980.

Lawton, Stephen. *Santa Barbara's Flying A Studio.* Santa Barbara, CA: Fithian Press, 1997.

Newland, James D., and La Mesa Historical Society. *La Mesa: Images of America.* Charleston, SC: Arcadia Publishing, 2010.

Stamp, Shelley. *Movie-Struck Girls: Women and Motion Picture Culture After the Nickelodeon.* Princeton, NJ: Princeton University Press, 2000.

Williams, Gregory L., and Gregg Hennessey, ed. "Filming San Diego: Hollywood's Backlot, 1898–2002," *Journal of San Diego History*, 48(2). Archived from the original on May 21, 2011; available at https://sandiegohistory.org/journal/2002/april/filming/.